The Hook
and
the Badge

THE HOOK
AND
THE BADGE

Life on the Waterfront

Jim Lynch

iUniverse, Inc.

New York Bloomington Shanghai

The Hook and the Badge
Life on the Waterfront

iUniverse books may be ordered through booksellers or by contacting:

iUniverse
1663 Liberty Drive
Bloomington, IN 47403
www.iuniverse.com
1-800-Authors (1-800-288-4677)

Because of the dynamic nature of the Internet, any Web addresses or links contained in this book may have changed since publication and may no longer be valid.

This is a work of fiction. All of the characters, names, incidents, organizations, and dialogue in this novel are either the products of the author's imagination or are used fictitiously.

ISBN: 978-0-595-42732-1 (pbk)
ISBN: 978-0-595-71047-8 (cloth)
ISBN: 978-0-595-87062-2 (ebk)

Printed in the United States of America

Introduction

The date was October 12, 1966. The ship that departed Boston several days earlier arrived after an uneventful voyage at the dock in Antwerp at 10:10 a.m. The five gangs of longshoremen who had been selected to unload her boarded the ship at 10:30 a.m. Hatch covers were removed and the men climbed down the ladders into the hold to start discharging a variety of cargo. The gang in hold #3 broke the custom's seal on the doors of the freezer compartment. Two in the gang pulled heavily on the large door handles while the others waited a few steps away. They all expected to see slabs of beef and lamb. They stopped dead in their tracks as their eyes focused on two objects directly in front of them. The rigidly stiff, frosted bodies stood straight for a few seconds as if they were going to walk out of the freezer, but then fell forward, crashing face first onto the deck. The faces of the gang, in unison, reflected surprise, awe and fear. After a few silent seconds, one of them hollered in Dutch to anyone on the upper deck, "Call the police."

But this story began long before these two bodies ever found their way to Antwerp.

CHAPTER 1

▼

1949 was a good year in the city of Boston. The war was over; the economy was beginning to improve. Veterans, most of them older than the average student, were attending college by the thousands. The G.I. Bill was making it happen. Homes were being built all over Boston and the suburbs. Young families were moving in as work was plentiful.

Boston had at least six newspapers, some with multiple editions. News read by talking heads wasn't upon us yet. Most people read two newspapers. It seemed that everyone could read. This is an observation, not a fact. Movies began to use cuss words, like damn and hell. Cleavage was becoming in style and bikinis weren't too far off, or on. Boston had two burlesque houses, the Old Howard and the Casino. Sally Rand was a big hit as a fan dancer. She moved those fans so fast that even though she was naked, you couldn't see much. But it was still titillating. Many men, whether business people or laborers, could be found there. The comedy performances were funny but most men were there to see skin. For Catholics, this was a confessional event.

The movie theaters filled the downtown, Washington Street area. Walking south you would see the marques for the Loews Orpheum, Keith Memorial, the Modern, the Paramount. On the opposite side of the street you had the RKO Boston. Beside movies, they had a live stage show that brought many famous stars, including Frank Sinatra, Spike Jones and His City Slickers, Kate Smith, a vocalist best known for her rendition of "God Bless America." You got goose bumps just listening to her sing that song. Sinatra was almost torn apart by fans on one of his appearances. Johnny Ray cried his way through many performances.

There were many types of restaurants and diners. Cafeterias were in full bloom. Places like The Waldorf, Hayes Bickfords, and The Englewood Diner were open 24 hours a day. Pizza pie was becoming very popular. The most famous pizza restaurant was the Pizzeria Regina located in Boston's North End. It's still there, in fact. Gradually, each neighborhood created its own favorite pizza place. Most were bars and sold whole pizzas only.

In Boston, work was plentiful with the minimum wage set at $0.75 an hour. Bread was 10 cents a loaf, potatoes 5 cents a pound, and an ice cream cone was a nickel. So was a candy bar. Many Bostonians went to work for a utility company, such as Boston Edison, Boston Gas, New England Telephone. It was easy to get employment, especially if your relatives worked at any of these places. Boston was filled with opportunities in the trucking industry, factories and the waterfront.

This was the work environment that Jackie Xavier Monyhan entered in 1949. Jackie was from the Valley, a section of Charlestown located close to the Massachusetts State Prison. Like his mother, Jackie had blue eyes, taking after her side of the family's Irish ancestors, and a good unblemished complexion, never having endured acne while growing up. Jackie was the youngest of eight. He had a suave way about him and he took a certain amount of pride in the way he looked. Starting in high school he used hair grease, liberally, on his beautiful head of jet black hair. The male fashion at the time was to give yourself the Robert Mitchum look; that is, self-confident in a defiant way. Smoking was in but Jackie was different, ever since Charlene, his first girl friend in high school, refused to go out with him any more because his clothes—as well as hers—started to reek of cigarette smoke. And she didn't like kissing him much anymore, either.

Besides good looks and personality, Jackie also turned out to be great in math. In any other community he would have been told to use this gift and get himself to college. But Jackie was content to compute baseball averages in his head while his friends tried to do them on paper. When he was older he would win many beers with this skill.

Most of his brothers were on the dole or worked for the city. His closest sibling, Paul, worked for Boston Edison. He got the job because he worked in Micky McGraw's election campaign for State Representative. His sister Jean, just one year older, was his favorite playmate when he was growing up, but that only lasted until he got more active in athletics. Jean shied away from the rough games then, preferring to play with her doll house that her father had discovered in the Charlestown dump. He had fixed it up, painted the thing to look like a Victorian house you would find lining Commonwealth Avenue in Boston. Jackie's older siblings were made up of one other sister, Irene, who was already in St. Bridget's

High School when Jackie was born, and four brothers, besides Paul. They already had their own friends and didn't bother much with the younger children, except at mealtimes when they would all crowd around the kitchen table. Jackie had fond memories of those early years—lots of noise. And the stories they could tell.

He had graduated from Charlestown High, after having been expelled previously from two Catholic High Schools—he just couldn't stomach the no-nonsense rules and regulations. He was a good athlete which had developed his trim figure. The girls loved him. He was an excellent quarterback and led Charlestown to two conference championships. In basketball he was an outstanding point guard, leading the league in assists and averaging twelve points a game. He played baseball because he was the only player who could play catcher. He pitched a few games after he trained Pete Boyle to catch.

Jackie's father, Matt, was a teamster and a weekend binge drinker; a very angry and hurtful man. It was a good thing for everybody that he was small and couldn't do much damage, drunk or sober. But he provided for his family, no one could deny him that. Jackie's mother, Bridget, was a very religious woman and tried to keep the family together and moving in the right direction. Unlike other wives in the area, she wouldn't allow Matt to hit her. He did once and was on the receiving end of a thrown frying pan. He sometimes would curse Bridget and threaten her, but he never laid a finger on her since that episode. He learned fast that he couldn't intimidate her. It was a good marriage, at least by Charlestown standards.

Charlestown is a northern peninsula belonging to the city of Boston. In 1949 it was connected to Boston by two bridges, the High Bridge and the Low Bridge. The High Bridge passed over Boston Harbor and connected the eastern end of Charlestown to the Italian section of Boston known as the North End. The Low Bridge, which was located further south, was strictly a railroad bridge. There was also a third bridge, the Prison Point Bridge, located on the southwest part of Charlestown, which spanned the Charles River and connected up with the city of Cambridge. On the northern fringe Charlestown abutted the city of Somerville. Charlestown had around 20,000 people, most of them employed as blue collar workers.

At that time the waterfront played a large part in the economic life of Charlestown. In addition to the Boston Naval Shipyard there were three major piers which handled cargo from all over the world. There were also two large sugar refineries located near the waterfront. Most of the housing was multiple dwellings. In fact, it was here, in 1939, that the first public housing project was built in America, on Bunker Hill Street. There were two famous tourist attractions.

These included the U.S. Frigate Constitution, the oldest active warship in the United States Navy, and the Bunker Hill Monument, an imposing landmark granite structure which pinpointed the site of one of earliest battles in the Revolutionary War. Within its scant, one square mile area, Charlestown could boast of three Roman Catholic Churches as well as 32 barrooms and cafes.

The population was fairly stagnant for many years. Many Townies, as they called themselves, were born here, went to school, worked, married, had kids and died here. But they couldn't be buried here because the only cemetery was occupied by colonists from the 18th century. If you were Catholic you probably would have been transported to Malden to be buried in the Holy Cross Cemetery. Most didn't know, or care, where the Protestants went. In fact, the Masonic Temple at Thompson Square, long considered a bastion of Protestantism, was considered off limits because mixing Catholics and Protestants was considered a bad idea. Ironically, it was located on top of the Charlestown Savings Bank, an institution very popular with area residents. Jackie had his first savings account there while growing up, putting his pennies in a Christmas club account.

There was good money to be made on the waterfront, but you had to hustle and be in the right place at the right time. The port of Boston used the "shape-up" system. There were a number of hiring spots throughout the city. In Charlestown there were the Hoosaic Pier and Wiggins Terminals. In South Boston there was the Army Base and one-half mile down Summer Street there was a hiring spot at Commonwealth Pier. There was also a hiring spot in East Boston, serving the U.S. Lines and the American Export Line.

There were about 1200–1400 men with union cards that were available for work. Some never worked. These were ex-cons who applied for a union card in order to help them get out of jail, stating that they had a union ticket to get a job. Jackie got his union card because his uncle Mike had been a longshoreman for 30 years. He was a member of local 799 which was the Charlestown local. There were two other locals in South Boston, 800 and East Boston 805. No matter which local you belonged to, you could work at any of the piers in the port. In a week you might work at two or three different terminals. The main goal was to get selected into a gang that labored for a stevedore who was employed by a major line that had two to three ships in port during one week. The busiest shipping lines were the Black Diamond, the Luckenback, the United States and the American Export. These ships would stay in Boston for two, maybe three days, occasionally more. That meant more work for everyone.

Around 1950 the International Longshoreman's Association (ILA) entered into a contractual agreement with the Boston Shipping Association on wages and benefits. The basic wage was $2.00 per hour with overtime of $3.00 per hour. A worker had to put in at least 400 hours to qualify for a pension year. Also, if he worked 700 hours, he would qualify for medical benefits which, at the time, were excellent.

Since Jackie was young and single he didn't pay much attention to these matters. All he was interested in was to make enough money to pay his board at home and go to some ball games and have a few beers with the guys. He won a lot of bets at the barroom playing blackjack because his math skills allowed him to count cards. This was before it became a no-no at the casinos. Little did he know that this would eventually bring him into a world of crime and corruption.

Jackie worked in Charlestown most of the time. He worked the "paper boats" which were owned by the Waterman Steamship Company. Their coastal route took them from New Orleans, Tampa, Savannah, Philadelphia, New York and Boston. Usually they carried large rolls of newsprint. The rolls were about six feet in length, about four feet in diameter and weighed 2000 pounds each. They were hoisted from the hold of the ship using clamps that stretched from one end of the roll to the other. The clamps tightened when the winch wires lifted the roll. It was not the safest way but the quickest, which was the important thing. There were one or two paper boats a week. This work, combined with Jackie's employment on the squid boats, provided him with a decent income. The squid boat was the nickname given to the vessels that traveled to and from Boston, Nova Scotia and Newfoundland. These ships arrived fully loaded, usually with wood and/or peat moss—but never squid—and were good for three days (24 hours) and two nights (four hours each night) work. Jackie worked in the hold on both lines.

CHAPTER 2

▼ —————————————

On the outside, Jackie appeared casual and nonchalant, but inside he had a burning desire to "be somebody," somebody important, someone whom people respected, looked up to. A person who people wanted to shake hands with. The problem was he didn't know in which direction to go. He had a few options, however. One was to work two jobs for a number of years, saving as much money as possible, then buy a bar and manage it himself. Maybe install a pizza oven to make a larger profit. Another way was to go to business school and get a degree in accounting because he was very strong in math. This had little appeal to Jackie, however, until he met Kathleen, a new girl in town. She moved to Charlestown from Lowell but she had actually been born in Moscow. Her parents were workers at the Swedish Embassy there. Her mother was from Sweden and her father from Arklow, Ireland. This genetic combination was very clear in her appearance. She was a ravishing beauty with brilliant blue eyes and light tanned skin. Her hair was strikingly blond. She worked for New England Telephone in Boston as an assistant to the head accountant. She also did some modeling on the side. She was 25 years old and lived with two female friends on Cordis Street in the Bunker Hill area of Charlestown. Her roommates liked to play the club scene and at times Kathleen tagged along. By coincidence, Jackie and Kathleen ended up at the same restaurant and bar in the South End. It was one of those nights that Jackie was traveling alone, trying to meet someone not from Charlestown. Why, he didn't know, but sometimes he got a feeling that in order for his life to change, he had to defeat the curse of being a blue-collar, second-class citizen from Charlestown. That particular night he had driven his car to a parking spot on Massachusetts Avenue, parked it, and just started walking around the area, stopping here and there for a drink or a coffee. He couldn't understand why he was doing this, but he had had these feelings before. Perhaps walking around in a strange area would help him feel different, that he could forget that he came from Charlestown.

It was a Thursday night with a light, cool breeze coming from the east, as usual, off the water. Not many people were out casually walking the streets this early in April. After what seemed like almost an hour he found himself at the corner of Columbus Avenue and Massachusetts Avenue standing in front of a place called The Checkered Bar and Restaurant. He put his hand in his pocket and felt a couple of bills and some change. As he was trying to make up his mind whether to go in, he heard from inside the sounds of Buddy Holly singing "Peggy Sue." It convinced him.

He was greeted warmly by a hostess who was very attractive, gave him a warm smile and said, "Good evening, how are you tonight?" She wore a tight, black clinging skirt and a revealing white blouse, along with mop of beautiful red hair which she liked to flaunt by frequently tossing it back to get it out of her eyes. Jackie wondered if it was her real color. With a ready smile she asked if he wanted a table or did he wish to sit at the bar. He chose the bar and she pointed to her left where there were some empty stools. Jackie followed her with his eyes as she turned and walked back to the hostess desk where two customers were waiting. She made sure that her backside rotated in time to the music, revealing her long infinite legs set atop a set of stiletto heels.

Jackie smiled to himself as walked to the bar, shifted around the back of the stool and sat down on the red leather seat. He pulled himself closer to the bar and pondered what he wanted to drink. He had had a few beers already but he had walked so much the effect had nearly worn off. But he didn't want to get drunk so he decided to stick to beer. The bartender, a gruff, no-nonsense, heavy-set guy who looked more like a bouncer in his black turtleneck and leather pants, asked what he wanted as he slapped a small, black and white checkered napkin down on the bar in front of him. Jackie ordered a beer—he didn't care what kind. In a few minutes Mr. Personality returned with a tall glass of beer.

"You want to pay now or start a tab?" he asked, as he placed the glass on the napkin.

"Tab," Jackie answered, without looking up at him. He would drink his beer slowly, another thing he was unaccustomed to, so that he would keep his tab low. This also gave him time to observe his surroundings. The bar was small but elegant and certainly the redhead did not diminish the décor. The music was coming from a juke box in the corner, positioned between the men's and ladies' rest rooms. Overall, the room was rather cozy, decorated in dark, vertical barn boards, separated by dark red panels. The lighting was appropriately subdued except for a few brighter overhead lights which were positioned over the cash registers. The glasses were black and white check to match the napkins. This also helped to create a club-like atmosphere that helped to calm Jackie down. He usually had a plan when he came into a new place like this, but tonight he decided to just see how it all played out.

He glanced around the room at the few round tables and noticed that there were two couples to his right and a few patrons to his left. He turned his chair slightly so he could see into the small dining room. Everything was casually elegant, including the people. He started to feel that maybe he was in the wrong place. Well, he thought, I don't have to stay long. Probably two drinks and he would be out of there.

The lounge was half full, which was surprising for a Thursday evening. Some couples were dancing on the small dance floor near the juke box but most were sitting at their tables, deep in conversation. He checked out the female clientele, pausing briefly at each table. At one table it looked like there was some kind of party, maybe a birthday, as an older woman was opening some small presents with everyone else at the table smiling and looking on. His glance shifted to a table near the corner of the room where three young women sat sipping their drinks. It looked like they were enjoying themselves, laughing and engrossed in each other. He was ready to move on when he noticed the blond sitting in the middle. Even from where he sat he could tell that there was something different about her. The glow of her eyes radiated all the way across the room. He swore that at some point they made eye contact and he instinctively moved his eyes in another direction. But her eyes were like magnets. He did his best not to turn and look again.

Wow, he said to himself, as he started to nervously chew his lip. *What is going on here?* He tried to regain his composure, tried to stop rotating his glass. Without really wanting to, he ordered another drink. He told the bartender he wanted a shot of Irish whiskey in a tall glass with one ice cube and nothing else. When the drink arrived he swallowed half of it in one gulp. The powerful Irish whiskey rushed to his stomach, causing a burning sensation and a feeling of joy all at the same time. The booze was doing what it was meant to do. He suddenly felt self-conscious and uneasy. *Well, dummy, what are you going to do now? Maybe walk out the door? Maybe order something to eat? Maybe go ask the attractive blonde to dance?* Jackie didn't like to feel awkward. If he were in another place, like a club in Charlestown, he wouldn't hesitate to ask her to dance because he would be half loaded and wouldn't care whether she accepted or not. Here, it was different. His thoughts drifted back to the number of times he had been rejected and the pain he had felt to his ego. More booze always killed that feeling, however. He tried to get himself to relax. *Stop chewing your lip!* One drink later he would make his move. Several minutes passed as he tried to get up his nerve to approach their table. He tried to not stare at her, but his eyes just couldn't keep away. If the blond had been alone, Jackie wouldn't have hesitated, but talking with three strange women at one table required that he have another drink. From out of nowhere he thought of his father's brother, his uncle Mickey, who had an old saying: when in doubt, punt or wait. So he waited some more.

Finally, getting up his nerve after finishing his last confidence-builder, he turned his bar stool toward the three women in the corner. To his surprise, the young women were putting on their coats. The blond turned slightly to her right and, he thought, gave him a smile. Not a big, heart-throbbing one but one that said, "Haven't I seen you someplace before?"

Jackie awoke with an awful taste in his mouth. He was scared to open his eyes. Slowly, he opened his eyes and saw that he was in the back seat of his car with no idea how he got there. He glanced down at his clothes and saw that his jacket was on the floor and his pants were halfway down to his ankles. "*Oh, shit*," he muttered out loud to himself. Then he noticed that there were scratch marks on his thighs and a red substance that looked like lipstick on his underwear. Turning his head he saw his wallet open next to the car's passenger door. As he reached over to pick it up he felt a stab of pain. It felt like a broken rib. He grabbed the wallet. Down deep he knew what to expect. His money was gone as well as his driver's license. As he stared at the empty wallet he heard several taps on the window. He turned sharply and saw the blue jacket and silver badge of a Boston policeman. "*Oh, shit*," he muttered again to himself.

As he groped frantically to pull up his pants he heard another tap and turned toward the window. He grasped the handle and rolled it down. Jackie looked again at the cop who had a grin on his face. It was then that he noticed that Paulie Campbell, Soup Campbell's brother, was staring at him, laughing his head off.

Jackie was lucky that day because Paulie hollered at him to pull up his pants and get the hell out of there, before the Super came along. Jackie quickly obeyed his orders and was soon speeding down Massachusetts Avenue, heading toward Washington Street. The elevated train above him screeched to a stop as he turned the corner, trying to remember the quickest way to drive to Charlestown.

He arrived back in Charlestown and parked his car near the Waldorf Cafeteria which was located in City Square. Relieved that he had gotten back safe and sound without hitting anyone or anything, he pressed his head against the steering wheel. He was one sick and suffering drunk. He had had to stop twice to throw up in the gutter. His throat hurt from the vomiting, his head was throbbing. He didn't know whether he wanted to live or die. It was about noontime so he had missed a pick-up for a job that would have lasted the weekend, at overtime pay.

As he looked across the street he had a choice. Directly in front of him was the Waldorf Cafeteria where he could get coffee and something to eat or, right next door, he could get a beer in the Morning Glory's Tavern. The latter, he reasoned, would help to put out the fires in his belly and head.

Jackie got out of his car and headed across the street. He still hadn't made up his mind whether to put out the fire or try to eat something. He thought about last evening. He had no intentions of getting drunk last night but he continued to drink even after he didn't want to. This had been happening a lot lately. The previous weekend had been another horror. On Sunday, he had ended up in New York City and had no idea how he had gotten there. His father told him that he was having alcohol blackouts. It seems that you could function normally but not remember it. By some miracle, you could drive and not get into an accident. Still he was suffering. He knew he had to get a fix, an upper, and then eat something.

He entered the Morning Glory about 12:15 p.m. It was overflowing with the lunch crowd. He walked to the bar, which was old and long and covered with cigarette butt scars and carvings left by the non-regulars. Regulars would never deface the altar of their existence. It was their code of religion. The Glory's smelled like many bars but more so. The smell of sawdust and dirt and ground-in liquor leaped from the floor and invaded your nostrils as soon as you came in the door. Other smells were indescribable, but if you had been there or in similar bars you would know what they were.

The Glory's was a bar for older folk. If you were under 50 you stood out and were treated with suspicion. A regular patron's first thought was that you were a plainclothes cop looking for a suspect. You could also be a lone shark looking for a client—to break his legs—or a hit man looking for the mark he was supposed to exterminate. Very few women drank here. Those that did were the older regulars. Others were women who had to use the ladies room, usually called the "john" or the "head", and felt that they had to buy a drink to pay the fee. Others were women who were lost or hookers looking for a pick-up. The Glory's also catered to the Navy, but the war was over now and there were few sailors around anymore.

Peter Fallon was behind the bar. He was a man about 55 of medium height with a tough, pock-marked, well-lined face. His hands were the size of tennis rackets. He had left Ireland after a battle with the Black and Tans. One soldier had been killed. There was now a price on the head of every man who had been in the shooting party. The price on Peter Fallon's was double because he had killed a tout or stool pigeon the year before. He paid a lot of money to stow away on a Dutch freighter which left the port of London. The ship docked in New York. From there Peter had made his way to Boston to take it easy for awhile. It was rumored that he still had influence in Ireland.

Jackie sat quickly at the bar, balancing himself on the stool, trying, not very successfully, to appear more sober than he was.

"Hi, Jackie. What'll it be today?"

"Old Thompson and a Ballantine," he mumbled. "Put it on my tab."

Peter moved like a machine and the drinks were in front of Jackie in less than thirty seconds. Jackie picked up the shot glass and noticed that his hand was shaking. The glass was filled to the top and whiskey was dribbling down over the rim. He knew he had to throw the whiskey down or Peter would notice. This was something he didn't want anyone to see. As the whiskey passed his lips and descended down his throat he felt that first stinging, burning sensation that always came with the first drink. Jackie just sat there, not moving. He wasn't sure it was going to stay down as his stomach was beginning to feel quezzie. He turned and was about to head for the men's room when his stomach relaxed. He turned back to the bar and chased the whiskey with half a glass of the ale. His system had slowed down and his hand was no longer shaking. Now was the second big decision. Should he have another round or should he go next door and get something to eat.

"Hey, Pete, can I borrow a few bucks to get me home? My car broke down and …"

Without saying a word Peter reached in his pants pocket and separated off two, five dollar bills and handed them to Jackie between two extended fingers. Jackie quickly took the bills without looking Peter in the eyes and shoved them in his jacket pocket.

"Thanks."

When Jackie looked up he saw the bartender was giving him a questioning look with raised eyebrows, asking silently if Jackie wanted a second round. Jackie could hold his hand up, palm forward, which meant he didn't want a refill, or he could tip his hand, indicating that he wanted another one. Jackie slowly raised his hand in the air.

It was morning because the brilliant sun streamed through the ripped window shade. The bright rays landed on Jackie's forehead; the heat adding to the pulsating pain already there. Slowly, he squinted through his eye lids, trying to focus through the haze. This also caused more pain. Jackie had suffered many levels of pain while playing football, but this was worse. It consumed every ounce of his body and ice or heat packs would not help. This was the pain of a helpless drunk who was isolated from the world and reality, then thrown into a world that was brought about by the bad choices he had made. He knew that it was all self-inflicted. A little voice kept telling him daily, *If you don't want to get hurt, don't get into the ring.* But after a few days, he felt fit and was ready to go back into that ring, thinking he could win this time. But, as usual, he didn't and here he was again, sick, unaware of where he was or how he had gotten there, and alone. The thought struck him like a lightning flash: *Am I really alone?* With the little energy he had, he turned to peek at the other side of the bed. Thank God, there was no one there. On the other hand, there was a look to the bed clothes like someone had indeed slept there. The pillow was ruffled with strands of black hair scattered upon it. There was also a faint smell of cheap perfume, almost like men's after shave lotion. Jackie shuddered and muttered out loud, "Oh, no!" thinking the worst. He gazed around the small room, looking for any other signs of who had been there. His eyes stopped at the little end table, probably bought at the Morgie. On the table, amidst the clutter of beer and vodka bottles, was a large metal ash tray, probably home made. A dozen extinguished cigarette butts were pressed to the bottom. He raised himself clumsily on one elbow and scrutinized the butts. Many of them had a bright red shade of lipstick imprinted on them. *Well, smart ass, I guess that means you were <u>probably</u> with a woman.* Then he added sarcastically, *I wonder if I had a good time.*

Slowly, he pulled himself up and swung his legs over the side of the bed. He sat there with his hands clutching the sheets, looking at the dirty, stained carpet. The room was hot and stuffy. He gazed around the room and noted how little furniture there was. The room had the look of a place where many one night stands had taken place. He didn't see a stove or a refrigerator. His clothes were on a chair next to his bed. His wallet was on the floor, empty of cash. He was afraid to walk to the window and look out, but he had to find out where he was.

As he was getting up, through his now pulsating headache, he heard footsteps outside the door, then a soft rap and a whisky-soaked voice speaking almost in a whisper.

"Time to get out. I gotta clean the room for the day people."

Jackie almost smiled despite his big head and thought, *Yeah, clean the room. You just pick up the empties and dump the ash trays, maybe open the window for some fresh air and straighten out the bed.* Jackie got dressed and was down the stairs and out the door in five minutes. He was pretty sure he didn't have his car last night, but, just in case, he quickly glanced around at the parked cars. *At least you didn't run over anybody on your way over here.* That made him feel a little better. As he slowly came out of his post-drunk haze he looked up and saw the ugly overhead tracks and realized that he was at the corner of Dover and Washington Streets. Directly in front of him were the steep stairs heading to the Dover Street T station. It was a gray day, just like his mood. *Looks like rain.*

He searched his pockets, finding enough change for the fare. He climbed the steps to the platform and waited. A few minutes later he heard the noise of the train before it turned the bend. It was half empty so he sat on the bench-like seats with plenty of room. With his head tilted back onto the window he closed his eyes and tried to think about last night's "adventure", most of which he couldn't remember. He was booze sick again which made him feel awful. *Why do you keep on doing this*, he asked himself? Last night, or was it the night before, he went with his friend Stevie O'Brien to have a few beers after the softball game at Hayes Square Field. They went to Rip McAvoy's, then the Old Timers and finally settled down at Scalli's Tavern in City Square.

Jackie knew that he was drinking too much. During the past year there were numerous times when he had blacked out and woke up in places that he didn't recognize or with people he didn't know. He was missing jobs, especially on the weekends. And his mother and sisters were on his back all the time. The question *What should I do?* kept running through his mind. He had been drinking since he was 13 years old. How do you change that? Every place he went—ballgames, wakes, parties—always involved drinking. Even Christmas Eve had become just another night to get drunk. Birthdays, anniversaries, Holy Communions turned into one more drunken party. He would go to these events with good intentions but after he had had a few drinks, most of the time beer, he couldn't or wouldn't stop. He kept on drinking until he passed out. He changed from the life of the party to the death of the party. But in his circle this wasn't unusual. Almost all of his friends lived like this. You worked hard, played hard, drank hard. That's what life was all about. But lately he had been thinking if that were really true. Was there another way to live? The bottom line was that he was sick and tired of being sick and tired. But then something happened that turned his whole world around.

He had worked for three days, having had no trouble getting picked for a gang. He had money in his pocket. He was tired and just wanted to relax, have a few drinks and go home early. It was Friday and he planned to stop in City Square, but at the last minute he changed his mind and went directly home. After he washed up he decided to lie down for a few minutes. As soon as his head hit the pillow he fell asleep. He stayed asleep until 10:00 p.m. Feeling better, he climbed out of bed, wondering what to do next. *Okay, smart guy, now what are you going to do? It's Friday night, the beginning of the weekend and here you are, at home with nothing to do.* The house felt stuffy and close. *To heck with this. I'm getting out of here.* Quickly, he changed his clothes, grabbed his jacket and hurried out the front door. Outside there was refreshing breeze coming in off the water. Feeling somewhat energized as he buttoned his coat he started to walk briskly down Main Street, headed for the Eight Bells Café. By the time he got to the Eight Bells his brain felt like it had a marching band parading around inside it. One side of his brain was saying, *go inside, have a drink, and relax.* The other was telling him, *don't go in, don't drink, stay sober tonight. Get a cup of coffee, then go home.* By the time he realized it, he was past the Eight Bells and standing in front of the Waldorf Cafeteria. Before he knew it he was entering the Waldorf and heading toward the counter. *I guess I'll get that cup of coffee after all, plus a pie a la mode.* As he turned from the counter with his tray, looking for a place to sit down, he recognized Tommy Woods by the faded blue watchman's cap and dark blue, pea jacket he always wore no matter what the weather. He was an older longshoreman, looking the part with broad shoulders and heavy lines on his tanned, leathered face. Tommy was a nice guy and had always treated Jackie fairly. To others he had a reputation for being snappish and grouchy but Jackie knew from experience while growing up that it was all a façade. Most of it was show, especially on the docks. It helped to keep the guys in line. Tommy was a gang boss for a few stevedores and was considered a good foreman.

He looked up as Jackie approached his table and said, "It must be a slow night when you're in this place at 10:30 on a Friday night, drinking coffee."

Jackie smiled as he sat down. "Ah, I was a little mixed up tonight and didn't know whether I wanted to drink or not, so I decided on some coffee."

"Good choice for you," replied Tommy seriously.

"What do you mean?" asked Jackie with a quizzical look on his face.

"Well, if you want to know the truth, I've heard some stories about your drinking. Some people think you've been hitting the sauce too much and it's catching up with you."

"Says who?" asked Jackie with a defiant touch to his voice.

"Come on, you know how stories on the docks don't sit quiet too long. I heard you had a little problem in the Glory's last week and then there was the incident in New York the week before that."

Jackie paused, sipped his coffee and calmed down. "Gee, Woodsie," he said, calling Tommy by his nickname. After several seconds of silence he added, "Are people really talking about my drinking?"

"Yeah, some people are, especially people who like you and don't want to see you end up a drunk."

"You mean like my father," Jackie added.

"I don't even know your father," said Tommy. "I mean the guys you see sleeping in the weeds, like Bonehead, Beef Stew, Johnny Meathead, those guys."

"Come on, you don't really think I could end up like that because I have a few drinks now and then," said Jackie, trying to sound convincing.

"Jackie, these guys didn't start out living in the weeds, they lived in homes just like you and they began drinking just like you. It was fun, it made them feel good, just like you feel, and they woke up in the morning with a colossal hangover, not knowing where they were or how they got there, just like you. The same questions ran through their minds, where's my car, was I in an accident, things that I'm sure you think about. This goes on for a while. Then they discover the morning drink. One morning they feel so bad that they open a bottle left over from the night before and they force down a gulp of booze. At first it might not stay there and they have to rush to the bathroom. Perhaps they vomit. Then they try it again, and again. Eventually it stays down and the shakes stop and the eyes clear and the world becomes livable again." Tommy paused for a sip of his coffee, then continued slowly, with a faint smile, "'Ah', you say to yourself proudly, 'I have found the cure. Life is good.'

"But life is not good because now the cycle goes around again. But I shouldn't be lecturing you like this. You still think you're having fun with booze and those things will never happen to you." Tommy sat back in his chair and stared at Jackie.

Jackie felt as if he had been hit over the head with a shovel. Why was Woodsie telling him all this? Did he really drink that much?

"How do you know so much about booze? I've never seen you drink."

"I know you haven't because I don't drink. Not any more. I haven't had a drink in years, but I still remember what it tastes like and what it can do to you."

Jackie sat for several seconds. "But if you don't drink, what do you do at parties or when you go out? How can you talk to people—or even ask someone to dance? I know I couldn't if I didn't have a few drinks in me first."

"It's easy once you try it," said Tommy. "I didn't think I could either but you find out that you can really dance and it's fun and you don't have to worry if someone is going to steal your drink or your change." With that, Tommy looked at his watch, pushed his dinner plate aside and got up to leave. "I've got to leave. I have to work tomorrow. I've got a job on the Black Falcon with Joe Cumphries."

"Me too. I mean, I'm working tomorrow at the Army Base with Tommy Logan. Before we leave, I have just one question for you, Woodsie. How did you stop drinking? Wasn't it hard? What did you do with your time? What do people do that don't drink? I just can't imagine a life without drinking."

Tommy sat down again and looked straight into Jackie's eyes. "Do you really want to know?"

Jackie returned home more confused than when he left. For some reason, he just didn't want to get drunk tonight. So what happened? He meets an older longshoreman friend who hasn't been drunk for over ten years and he tells him that the way to do it is not to take the first drink, go to meetings for drinkers called Alcoholics Anonymous and ask a power greater than himself, call it God if you want, to help you stay away from a drink of alcohol. Then he tells him that it is not a religious program even though God is mentioned frequently. It is a spiritual program, he says. Jackie climbed into bed but didn't fall asleep for an hour. He had a lot to think about.

Jackie awoke feeling very strange for a Saturday morning. His throat wasn't dry, his eyes weren't bloodshot, his stomach wasn't grumbling and his mouth didn't feel as if he had chewed on a piece of cotton all night. And he wasn't thirsty. He didn't have that unquenchable thirst that he always had on Saturdays or any morning after a night of drinking. Maybe he would meet Woodsie again tonight and go to one of those meetings with him, as he suggested.

CHAPTER 3

▼

Jackie enjoyed the feeling of not drinking as much. It was so nice to wake up in the morning without a hangover, without the feeling of nausea and rushing to the bathroom to hug the toilet bowl. He didn't miss the incredible thirst that could never be satisfied unless it was a drink of alcohol. Some called it a taste of the hair of the dog that bit you. He knew where he was last night and where his car was. Plus, he knew it wouldn't have any new unexplained dents. But most of all, it was the freedom that he enjoyed most. As long as he didn't drink he could go any place, do anything (of course, nothing illegal), and talk to people without covering his mouth, afraid they might smell the booze. He didn't have to build his day around the question "When am I going to get a drink?"

It wasn't easy but it was simple idea: just don't take that first drink. When you get up out of bed in the morning, get on your knees, then go the next 24 hours without a drink and then return to your knees at night. There were a few AA meetings in Charlestown and Malden, but meetings were now starting to take place in every section of the city and suburbs. Even though he went to AA meetings, at first with Woodsie, then more often by himself, he was still having trouble staying away from that first drink. But refusing that first drink was starting to get easier, one day at a time, one day at a time.

It was during this time that he met Kathleen. His buddies were having a bachelor party for Tony Spag, one of the few Italians that lived in Charlestown. Tony could drink like a fish but you would never notice it. He could fight like a demon, too. This also helped him become part of the crowd at the bars.

The bachelor party began at the Eight Bells on Chelsea Street. Jackie met them there. He decided to have one drink. As the crowd was leaving to head over to the next party at the Beacon Club in Everett, Jackie decided at the last minute to stay for a while at the Eight Bells. His friends Stevie O'Brien and Paul Murphy were really angry at him because he wasn't going with them. Jackie said he might meet them later on. Since Jackie had cut down on his drinking, most of his friends had accepted it except Stevie and Paul. Both said that Jackie always drank just like they did and they didn't think that either of them had a problem.

Joey Mons was on the bar that night. He and Jackie had been friends for years, both on and off the waterfront. Joey was Italian, 51 years old and stood 5'11", weighing 180 pounds. He had been an amateur boxer while in his teens. With a dark complexion, with deep brown eyes and arms which were covered with curly black hair, he could have been a lady's man but he firmly believed in family and religion. He never strayed from that belief. Jackie had met him during his first year working as a longshoreman. Jackie was only 17 and had no idea what he was doing during those early weeks on the waterfront. It was all on the job training. One day Jackie was working on an East Indian ship, discharging bags of coffee, when Joey first introduced himself.

"Let's team up. Here, I can help you with these bags. You do it like this; you take a rope sling and spread it like this on the deck. The most important thing is to lay the sling right, so when the bit tightens up, it will be on the top of the load at the right place." Then he told Jackie to grab one end of a bag while he grabbed the other. They swung the bag and placed it on top of the sling. "Placing the first bag is the next most important thing." Together, they made up a load of the coffee beans, three bags long and three bags high. It lifted out of the hold without any problem. And so began their close friendship where Jackie was the student and Joey was the teacher.

Because of the "shape up" system, they were partners most of the time. This continued for the next five years until Joey was injured one day while they were working on a lumber ship. They were on Castle Island. It was a cold, blustery day in February. A freezing rain the night before had made the walking dangerous. Joey was attempting to get out of the way of a falling 2 x 4 when he slipped on the icy deck. He landed on his head and hip, passing out. When he awoke he was in the Carney Hospital with his lower body encased in a plaster cast and his wife standing over him. Her eyes were red but she had stopped crying. She leaned over and gave him a kiss.

Joey remained in the hospital for twelve days. When he was released he returned home with half his body still in a cast. Healing was slow. When the cast was removed he went through weeks of physical therapy. But it was clear that Joey would never work on the docks again.

Jackie would visit Joey and try to cheer him up. "You lucky son of a bitch, you'll be on workingman's comp and make a barrel of money while doing nothing. How lucky can you get?"

Joey would smile but it was easy to tell that this wasn't what he wanted. Finally, during November of that year Joey was placed on the permanent disability list and granted a small pension.

Joey was feeling very depressed when George Monroe, the owner of the Eight Bells Café on Chelsea Street, offered him a bartender job for a few weeks. Joey had already worked there a few years ago when the longshoremen had been on strike. Joey said that he would talk it over with his wife and let George know the next day. After supper that evening, Joey presented the idea to Marcie and it didn't take long before they both agreed that it was the best thing for Joey, and the family. The few weeks turned into years of steady employment.

Jackie sipped his beer while Joey Mons peered at him strangely. Nobody in Charlestown sipped beer, especially Jackie. He could feel Joey's eyes on him and it made him feel funny. Quickly, he tossed back the glass and swallowed the last few ounces and ordered another one. Joey drew a draft of Bally Ale and as a joke he stuck a straw in it and walked down to Jackie with a sly grin on his face.

Jackie laughed as Joey set the glass in front of him. Sarcastically, Jackie hollered "There goes your tip."

Joey retorted, "You cheap son of a bitch. You young guys never leave one anyway, unless you have a pocketful of pennies."

Jackie went along with Joey and started drinking the ale through the straw. He made the ale last about 15 minutes, then stood and took a dollar from his billfold and placed it on the bar and said, almost in a whisper but as seriously as possible, "Hey, you embarrassed me, Joey, in front of all those people, so I have to leave a tip."

Joey faked throwing a bottle at him and screamed, "Get the hell out of here so I can go home and get abused by my old lady." Joey Mons was a happy-go-lucky guy who knew how to be a good bartender. Good with the customers, honest to the management. There were only a few customers left in the Eight Bells when Jackie turned to leave. "Hey, before you leave, big spender, come over here a minute. I want you to meet somebody."

Jackie followed Joey as he walked to the other end of the bar. Joey pointed to a young man who had a mixed drink in front of him. "I want you to meet my younger brother, Sal; just got himself discharged from the Marine Corps. He served two years in Korea and has a Purple Heart to prove it." As Joey smiled at his brother he added, "He was considered one of the top sharpshooters in his unit."

Jackie walked up to Sal and they shook hands. "Nice to meet you, Sal."

Sal answered, "Same here."

Sal was quite a bit younger than Joey, with angular features and a lighter complexion. His hair was dark brown but very short. It looked like he had gotten a haircut just before leaving the Corps. He returned his hands to wrap around his drink. It was easy to spot the military ring on his left ring finger. Jackie also noticed that he had on a Boston College jacket.

"Right now he's looking for a job," Joey said.

"I guess the Marines didn't prepare you for the ordinary working world," said Jackie.

"They sure didn't," replied Sal looking at Jackie, as he drew from his shirt pocket a fresh pack of Camels. He hit the package several times on the bar to settle them down. He opened the pack and withdrew one, then bent toward Joey who had a match already burning for him. After taking a heavy drag and blowing it toward the ceiling, he dropped the pack on the bar in front of him. "I've got a few things lined up, a few people to see."

"Where are you living?" asked Jackie.

Joey laughed and said, "Get this. He's living with me 'til he gets back on his feet."

Sal grinned while looking at his brother. "Yeah, and to think we used to fight all the time when we were kids. Joey was the big brother so I had to let him win."

"Get out of here," said Joey as he threw a fake punch at his brother. Sal played along, raising his arms while ducking the punch, a cigarette dangling from his lips.

"Glad to see you guys finally getting along. I hardly see my brothers any more. You're lucky."

"Yeah, we know, but I still have to look after him, you know," said Joey with a smile.

Jackie left the bar in good spirits. Then suddenly the thought hit him. *What am I going to do now?* He looked across the street and all he saw were barrooms: Jack's Café, Scalli's Tavern, The Morning Glory's. Out of place and nestled in between was Dot's Diner. He considered going there for a cup of coffee, but reconsidered, remembering that it was Saturday night and the diner would be like fight night at the Boston Garden. Forget it, he said to himself. That left the Waldorf Cafeteria at the corner, so he walked the short distance to the entrance. As he walked past the large plate glass window that stretched the length of the restaurant he had the feeling that someone was staring at him. Involuntarily, he turned to his right and looked into two beautiful blue/green eyes that he seemed to remember from somewhere. He kept walking and pushed the door open into the cafeteria. Something flashed through his mind telling him, yes, she was the girl he saw at the lounge in the South End some time ago. *What is she doing here? Who is she with?* It was not only the color of her eyes but the laser-like effect they had on his heart and soul. *This is unreal.* He had never felt like this before.

Jackie walked slowly toward the counter, turning his head from left to right as if looking for a friend. He knew where the young woman with the gorgeous eyes was sitting. She was with a pretty dark haired woman who looked about the same age. Jackie walked along the food counter and spotted the apple pie a la mode, which was the Waldorf's specialty, and a cup of coffee. He paid at the register and then walked down the middle aisle, glancing around as if looking for an empty table. When he was two tables away from them, he cut across the aisle so he was in front of the two women. The brunette looked up and with a sarcastic smile on her face asked, "Are you lost?"

Jackie was taken back by the question but decided to play along and replied, "Kinda."

The blonde looked straight into his eyes and with a grin said, "Well, if you're someone we can't trust, move on, if not, sit down."

They had sat at a table for four. He sat next to the dark haired one so that he could look at the blonde. He said the first thing that came into his head.

"They sure have good pie here." He put sugar in his coffee and stirred while thinking what to say next.

"Yeah, you're right. We just decided to split one. Keeping our figures, you know," said the brunette. "My name's Marilyn and my friend is Kathleen."

"My name is Jackie. You live around here?"

"We're both from Charlestown."

"Yeah, me too."

Well, he thought, what do I do now? It was so much easier to be social when you were half in the bag with loads of confidence.

Slowly, he began to eat his pie when Kathleen said, "How come you're not out gallivanting tonight with the guys?"

Looking across at her, trying to avoid staring, he replied, "I just didn't feel like it tonight."

"Getting old," retorted Marilyn.

"Naw," he answered. "Maybe just getting wiser."

Kathleen jumped in quickly saying, "You look familiar. Didn't we see you at a club in the South End some time ago? It was kind of an expensive place."

Jackie knew for certain that he had seen them but he wasn't too quick to answer.

"Probably," he said, "but that must have been quite awhile ago." He tried to focus on the present but he kept thinking about Kathleen, feeling nervous just to be sitting near her. He continued to eat his pie and ice cream, doing it more automatically than actually enjoying it. His coffee was getting cold.

He could feel the high energy flowing from her body to his. He wondered if she felt the same. She was so different from any woman he had known. No other woman had ever had this effect on him before. It was difficult to avoid looking at her face, which, after a few minutes, he could describe in his sleep. Her long hair to her shoulders was really auburn but looked blonder in the light. As he glanced at her eyes he could see that they were as much green as blue. Her smile came easily and he started to relax. He finally took a sip of his coffee.

Jackie tried to bring Marilyn into the conversation but he could sense that she knew all his focus was on Kathleen. He tried talking about sports which Kathleen knew all about but Marilyn knew very little. Finally he asked them where they worked.

Marilyn answered. "We both work at New England Telephone in the accounting department, on State Street in Boston. Do you know where that is?"

Jackie answered, "Sure, I know Boston pretty well. I work in the city, too."

"Oh, where?" jumped in Kathleen.

"At the Boston Army Base and Commonwealth Pier," said Jackie.

"Do you work at the fish pier?" asked Marilyn.

"No, I work at the Hoosaic docks most of the time."

"You work in a lot of different places," said Marilyn. "How come?"

Between bites of apple pie Jackie was able to answer. "The ships dock at different piers, so we have to go there to get hired. That's where the shape-up or pick-up takes place," answered Jackie.

"How does that happen?" asked Kathleen.

Jackie had calmed down now, enjoying the conversation. To his surprise, his apple pie and ice cream were all gone and his coffee cup was empty.

"That's where the hiring boss, or stevedore, picks the men to work the ship. Those that he knows he calls by name, otherwise he points to men that he wants."

"That's kind of weird," said Marilyn laughing.

"It's an old custom dating back to the early days of shipping," Jackie answered, as he pushed his plates away, remembered to use his napkin, then rested his elbows on the table. "At that time, when a cargo ship was sailing into port, the captain of the ship would stand on the bow and holler, 'Any men along the shore who want to work?' Those that wanted a job would then line up at the ship's pier where the captain would pick them out. That's where the name long-shoreman came from. Since most of the cargo was carried or rolled off the ship, the captain would select the biggest and strongest looking men."

After a short pause Kathleen looked at her watch. "That's enough about long-shoremen tonight. It's after my bedtime. I've got to get up early tomorrow."

As the three got up to leave, Jackie wondered what he could say so that he could see Kathleen again. It was Kathleen who answered it for him.

She smiled and looking directly at Jackie said, "We can continue this conversation some other time."

"Anytime is fine with me," said Jackie quickly. Jackie found himself smiling back at her.

As he walked home that night, he realized that he hadn't even thought about wanting a drink.

CHAPTER 4

▼

Jackie walked down Chelsea Street, headed toward the pick-up spot at the Hoosaic Pier. It was a Monday and work was plentiful. He crossed the street into the hiring area. In his mind he was trying to determine which job would give him the most work. He knew that the paper boat could be three days work but no overtime. On the other hand, the squid boat, the S.S. Newfoundland, would probably last three days and two nights. That is where he headed.

The hiring boss was Happy Hogan. Jackie usually got hired in the second gang when Happy was in charge. This was also true today. He was teamed with Pete Foley, a man twenty years older than Jackie, strong as a bull and a smart worker. Most gangs consisted of 21 men. Four worked on the deck running the hoisting winches and giving signals to the nine who worked on the pier. Another eight men were either discharging or loading cargo directly into the ship's hold. Today they were discharging bales of wool using sharp cargo hooks. These were forced into the wire band that was strapped tightly around each bale. Four bales were hoisted at a time. Usually there were 22–25 hoists an hour, depending on the skill of the winchmen. When the bales landed on the dock, they were unhooked by a team of two to three men called landers. The other dock men used long-armed two-wheelers to bring the wool into the warehouse where clerks laid out spots where the bales would be placed temporarily.

Jackie and Pete grabbed some wool hooks as they descended and passed two sets of hooks to the other holders, Sammy the Limp, Joey-the-Shoes Connolly, Mike Sligo, Joe Green, Butch O'Donnell and Artie Shaw. The guys worked well together and the cargo moved quickly out of the hold. The men talked about the news, sports, or waterfront gossip. The work was dangerous so you had to keep alert. A hook could slip or a strap could snap, dropping the bale back into the hold. This was an experienced gang of men and Jackie felt good working with them.

It took about two hours to discharge the wool. The next items to be brought up were bales of peat moss. These were discharged by piling them neatly into a rope sling which was then hoisted out onto the dock by the winchmen. They worked in pairs so there was always a load ready to be hoisted out. Jackie and Pete worked well together. They put their load together quickly, and then rested. The work continued until twelve o'clock when everyone climbed out of the hold to go to lunch. Pete and Jackie walked up to the Doherty's Tavern to get a few beers and a couple of hotdogs.

Jackie and Pete returned to work at 1:00 p.m. They discharged peat moss for the remainder of the day. They were going to work that night so they left for supper at 5:00 p.m., would return at 7:00, then work till 11:00. This was called a "half night" and they would be paid time and a half for the work. Jackie planned to eat dinner at the Waldorf in City Square, then go watch a softball game at Hayes Square Playground. He would be back to work in plenty of time.

Jackie enjoyed any type of sports and played softball two nights a week whenever he could. Working as a longshoreman kept him in good shape because there was a lot of bending and lifting. Except for beer, he kept most things in moderation. Thinking of the beer brought him back to remember last Friday. He had gone out for a few with his friends and ended up waking up drunk in some strange bar, not knowing how he got there. He had started out with friends and ended up alone. Well, he thought, next time I'll just have to be careful. He was still attending AA meetings and serious about wanting to quit.

When he got to the park after dinner the game was in the second inning. The Horseshoe Tavern was playing the Morning Glory's. The score was 2 to 0 in favor of the Glory's. The Horseshoe Tavern was at bat and Skinny Barret was at the plate. He was far from skinny now. He picked up his nickname at the age of 12 when he was thin as a rail. Later, at 18, he entered the Marine Corps and turned his life around, especially his body. He grew to 6'2" and weighed 210 lbs with very little fat. He surprised everyone when he returned to school and graduated from Boston College with honors. He now taught at Boston College High School and was assistant football and basketball coach. He was also the head coach of baseball. He still lived in the same house that he had been raised, although both his parents were dead. Jackie and he had been good friends for years. Skinny was always encouraging Jackie to go to college, but Jackie was making too much money on the docks to even want to make the change.

Jackie glanced at his watch and got up to leave as Skinny smashed a home run over the center field fence, the deepest part of the park. As he rounded third base he looked Jackie's way and gave him a "what do you think of that" kind of wink. Jackie grinned and gave him a wave as he turned and walked through the fence. He walked quickly along Chelsea Street. This would take him directly to the Hoosaic Docks where the Newfoundland was moored. He didn't look forward to working nights, but the money was good and he was trying to save a few bucks. He had a car, a dazzling '42 Chevy, but he couldn't afford to put it on the road yet. He thought that at least this way he couldn't get into any car accidents.

It was 6:55 p.m. when he walked up the gangplank of the Newfoundland. He was the last worker to descend the ladder. As soon as he hit the lower deck it was time to start. The first load was hoisted at 7:08; the half-a-night had begun. Jackie thought that it would be an easy night and settled in.

As Jackie and Pete made up their first load, Jackie noticed that Joey-the-Shoes Connolly and Butch O'Donnell were both drunk. Butch was the drunker of the two. It was open knowledge that both worked part-time for the Hayes-McCormick Gang. But this didn't prevent them from disliking each other, especially when they were drinking. The trouble began when Butch started talking especially loud about the new workings of the Gang. Joey told him to shut up and pay attention to what he was doing. Butch replied "Don't you tell me to shut up, you asshole."

As they moved toward each other a booming voice from the top deck hollered down, "Both of you shut up and get the fuck back to work or get your coats and get off this ship."

Pete and Jackie moved toward the pair to act as peace-makers, but Butch looked at them and said, "Stay the fuck out of this you two shitbirds." This seemed to bother Pete who made a move towards Butch.

Quickly, Jackie moved in front of Pete, saying, "Let it go. You don't win with these guys even if you do. It's not worth it."

Ten years ago Pete would have handled Butch easily, but now he was a father of three children and much smarter. He heeded Jackie's advice, stepped backwards, turned and faced the other way.

By this time Happy Hogan was again hovering over the hatch yelling, "If I don't get a load in two minutes, the both of you will be fired and don't think you'll ever get a job from me again, regardless of who your fucking friends are." The work resumed but the air remained as tense as a thunderstorm ready to explode.

The rain started about 8:30 and moved quickly from a gentle downpour to a driving rain. The boss hollered down to the men in the hold, "Come up and hang a tent. They don't want the coffee on the next deck to get wet. Hurry up."

Butch headed for the ladder with enthusiasm because he knew that they wouldn't reopen the hatch for the rest of the night and he would be able to get in a few hours drinking and get paid for it, too. As Jackie climbed out of the hatch Butch was half way down the dock, headed for a barroom. They wouldn't see him anymore tonight. Thank God, Jackie said to himself. It was almost nine o'clock. Jackie headed for the Waldorf to get a cup of coffee and a slice of apple pie. As he was going to cross Chelsea Street he heard some shuffling of feet behind him. He turned quickly and saw Joey-the-Shoes' fist headed toward his face. He raised his left arm to block the punch and squared up to throw a counter punch that hit Joey's ear. He shoved his left hand into Joey's jaw and drove his right hand into his stomach. Joey stumbled back and fell to the sidewalk directly in front of Jack's Café. A few patrons came to the door to see what was going on. Once they saw Joey on the ground, semi-conscious, they strolled back into the café. In their eyes the fight was over. The guy left standing was the winner. Rah, Rah, let's go back to our drinking.

Jackie stood close to Joey but not close enough for him to grab his legs. He yelled, "What the hell are you doing? I have no beef with you and you shouldn't have any with me."

Joey-the-Shoes stared at Jackie through tired and bloodshot eyes. As he started to get himself up he whispered, "This isn't over. Once I tell Tommy, he'll be all over you."

Jackie's anger rose at the mention of Tommy Hayes' name. He was about to hit Joey again but something stopped him. He knew Tommy from high school but he was a different guy now. Instead of walking to the Waldorf, Jackie changed direction and headed toward Main Street where he lived in a small apartment near Pleasant Street. His thoughts, however, kept returning to Tommy Hayes.

CHAPTER 5

▼

It was past eleven when Jackie opened his apartment door, entered, and tossed the keys on the small table that was next to the door. He snapped on the light and headed toward the bathroom. When he finished washing up he walked into his bedroom. He kicked of his shoes and then looked in the mirror. He felt as exhausted as he looked. He slumped into bed without taking off his clothes. Within a minute he was asleep. All night his dreams were filled with scenes of violence and mayhem. Jimmy McCormack and Tommy Hayes were yelling at him, "You work for us or you're going to suffer a lot of pain. You need us or you're going to get hurt real bad."

Jackie woke from this frightful sleep at 5:30 a.m., his clothes soaked in sweat. He rose quickly and turned on the gas under the kettle as he headed toward the bathroom. After leaving his clothes in a pile on the floor, he jumped in the shower, even though the water was only slightly warm, spitting out a few swears at the landlord, again. He dried off quickly and with a towel round his waist, ran into the kitchen. He placed a tea bag in his Red Sox cup and poured the scalding hot water from the kettle over it. He allowed it to brew for about two minutes, then threw the bag into the sink. Holding his cup he walked back to the bedroom, went to his bureau and took out a bright blue flannel shirt and a pair of heavy work pants. It was early spring but it was still going to be a cold day. He had to be careful not to overdress. Working in the hold could bring on a heavy sweat so you had to dress appropriately. He looked at the few jackets he had in the closet and chose a brown and black beach jacket that was warm but very flexible. He checked the gas stove twice to make sure it was off—a carry-over from living with his mother as she feared that the house would blow up if the gas had been left on—then walked over to the closet. He found his cargo hook and slipped it between his belt and pants so that the pointed end was pressed against the leather belt. The last thing he did was force his work gloves into his pockets and push his gray scally hat on to his head. After locking the door he jumped down the three steps and landed on Main Street. It was 7:30 a.m. The cool air hit him in the chest but it felt good and he took a deep breath. He had plenty of time but he broke into a slow jog with the intention of getting another cup of coffee. He crossed Main Street, went into the Waldorf and ordered coffee and toast to go. Then he was on his way to the Hoosaic Pier where the squid boat was waiting.

The men who were hired yesterday would return today and begin work. The time keepers would make the rounds and note who was there and who was absent. Afterwards, Happy would go to the head of the pier and hire replacements. It was 8:00 a.m.; work began. The giant tent that had covered the hatch overnight was removed by the boom, hoisted into the air and placed on the waterside of the deck. Jackie and his partner were the first to go down the ladder. Butch O'Donnell and Joey-the-Shoes Connolly were conspicuously absent but no one really cared. They continued to discharge the peat moss until 10:00 o'clock. Jackie and Pete were glad that Butch and Joey didn't show up. They would have been hung-over and dying to get into an argument with anyone. It wasn't that Jackie and Pete were afraid of them, just that it was dangerous. You never knew when those guys would be carrying a weapon and they weren't afraid to use them. Their absences made the morning more pleasant and the time passed quickly.

After the peat moss was finished, they began discharging casks of scotch whiskey, uncut, probably 140 proof. They had to be handled carefully. Clamps were used to hook up four at a time and they were hoisted out of the hold onto the dock. Then they were rolled inside the warehouse by the dock gang. There were 125 casks to be unloaded, so this would take the rest of the morning. Most would go to the Mr. Boston Distillery in South Boston.

Immediately at noon, work stopped and the men went to lunch. Jackie and Pete headed for the Waldorf, moving fast so they wouldn't have to wait too long in line. As they crossed Chelsea Street, Jackie noticed a black Lincoln parked in front of the Eight Bells Tavern. Without looking at the driver, Jackie knew that Tommy Hayes was sitting in the passenger seat. There weren't many black Lincolns in Charlestown.

As they walked past the Lincoln, the passenger side window was lowered and a soft, calm voiced said, "Hey, Jackie, could I talk to you. It won't take long, I know you're working."

Jackie stopped and said "Sure, Tommy." He turned to Pete, "Go ahead, I'll be there in a minute. Save me a seat."

As Pete cautiously walked away, Tommy opened the car door and stepped out onto the sidewalk. He had on a short, black leather jacket over a grey sport shirt and dark grey cuffed slacks. He put out his right hand. Jackie shook it with a little apprehension. Tommy smiled and said, "Relax, I heard about Joey-the-Shoes and you last night. You did the right thing. Joey can be a pain in the ass when he's drunk." With a sly grin he added, "He was so bad last night that his old lady had him pinched. We bailed him out this morning. So, how are things going with you? You look in great shape."

"Things are good," Jackie replied with somewhat of a forced smile. "Yeah, I cut down on the drinking and that seems to help keep the weight down, too. And working in the hold of a ship is good exercise. You know, all of the lifting and stuff."

Tommy smirked and said, "Be serious, Jackie. I have a hard time picking up a cup of coffee, never mind a bag of it. But I can see what you mean." Tommy looked Jackie square in the eyes, bent over toward Jackie's ear and said softly, "You know that job offer is still open. It wouldn't involve any heavy hitting or stuff, just card games, maybe a few rounds of blackjack with a few friends. You could help count out the profit. I know I could trust you. You can bow out any time you want, no strings attached." He leaned back on his car and folded his arms across his chest, waiting for an answer.

Jackie shook his head, saying, "Thanks, Tommy, but not just yet. I have too many things on my plate right now."

Tommy extended his hands with his palms toward Jackie. "No pressure. I just wanted to remind you that it was still there. And look, don't worry about Joey-the-Shoes or Butchie. I've warned them to bug off." Tommy turned and got back in the Lincoln.

As the car door closed, Jackie said, "Thanks, Tommy, I appreciate that." Slowly, the Lincoln pulled out from the curb, then the driver gunned the engine. The car disappeared around the corner. Jackie continued walking toward the Waldorf. What was that all about, he thought.

Pete looked at him curiously as he entered the restaurant. "So, what goes? Was it about last night?"

Jackie forced a smile and said, "No, he was congratulating me on the bet I won from Joey Mons on the Celtics. He wanted to make sure I got my money up front, about $350."

"That's good," said Pete. "I was starting to worry."

Jackie turned toward the counter and quickly changed the subject, "I think I'll get a bowl of beef stew and a coffee. That shouldn't take long. I'm hungry."

Jackie and Pete returned to work at one o'clock. All the barrels of whisky had been discharged. The next items were in the pad locked room, located in the after end of the hatch. One of the ship's mates descended the ladder, searched for the right key and opened the pad lock. According to the checker's manifest, the locker contained cases of vodka, whiskey, wine, cans of shrimp and Norwegian sardines. This was a looter's paradise, especially if the mate didn't stay in the hold to safeguard the cargo. Stealing on the waterfront was almost a given. A few stole more expensive items but there was very little pilfering on a large scale. Some men wore jackets with deep and wide inside pockets that could hold a few cans or a quart bottle of vodka or whiskey. One of the workers would try to distract the mate or watchman while another would take a case of whiskey or tuna and hide it in another area of the ship's hold. During the rest of the shift each man in the gang would have an opportunity to take one or more and stuff it in his jacket.

The first item discharged tonight was cartons of shrimp. They were placed on a cargo loading board three rows across, six rows long and six cases high for a total of 108 cartons per load. Behind these cases were cartons of wine from France, with 12 bottles in each carton. When they reached the wine Skippy Ward walked to the other end of the hatch and lit a cigarette. The ship's mate walked over to him yelling, "Hey, put out that cigarette!" While this was going on Smokey Johnson grabbed a case of wine and hid it under his jacket which was lying on top some of the cargo. Skippy slowly put out the cigarette and returned to work. A few hours later the locker was completely discharged and the mate left the hold. At the end of the afternoon, each man of the eight man crew took a bottle with him, including Jackie and Pete. One of the fringe benefits of being a longshoreman.

CHAPTER 6

▼

When he was younger, Tommy Hayes was very intelligent, quiet, introverted. Born and raised in Charlestown, he was doted on by his mother. His father was a long-haul truck driver. He was a good student, caused few problems and even won spelling bees and essay contests. Unlike many teenagers, he didn't play sports or associate with girls. His younger brother, Norman, idolized him. When his older brother, Bernie, was killed by a drunk driver, Tommy became more withdrawn and went into seclusion. After two months of this behavior he joined the Marine Corps and left immediately for boot camp. Most people in town forgot about him.

He completed his Marine Special Forces training and was ready for active duty. World War II was still raging. Several changes had taken place with Tommy. He learned from the older recruits what girls were all about. He also started smoking and drinking a few beers. Actually, it was these activities that led him to discover women. After a few weeks, Tommy was a regular at the bars and the brothels. He appeared to be very quiet and reserved, but many people misread him to their sorrow. Tommy was filled with hatred and anger and the slightest provocation could trigger a vicious beating that could end in serious injuries. After one particularly nasty confrontation in a bar he was summoned to the office of the Marine Commander. Tommy was somewhat anxious because he imagined the worst. He also wondered whether he had gotten one of the many girls he knew pregnant and she had reported him. Colonel Baskin met Tommy at the door and they saluted. Then the Colonel shook his hand and led him to the seat next to his desk. The other seat in the room was occupied by Lt. Ransom, a 20 year veteran and holder of the Silver Star and the Purple Heart. Both looked very serious. Colonel Baskin began the conversation by asking Tommy what he thought of the Marine Corps. Tommy was surprised and blurted out, "Sir, am I in any kind of trouble?"

Colonel Baskins smiled slightly. "No, no, even though you should be more careful. You're not in any trouble. It's just that we have a special assignment and we think you might be the right soldier for it."

Tommy relaxed and asked, "What kind of an assignment?"

Colonel Baskins looked even more serious. "What we talk about from now on doesn't leave this room, whether you take the assignment or not."

Tommy quickly answered, "Yes, sir. I understand completely."

Colonel Baskins shifted in his chair and stared at Tommy. "You will be doing a great service for your country, but only a few people will know about it and the American people will never know. You won't receive any medals or recognition but if completed successfully, you will be considered a hero in our eyes. Shall I go on, Tommy?"

Tommy maintained eye contact with the Colonel and said emphatically, "Yes, sir."

"Looking at your training record, we see that you have received high marks in combat training, especially hand-to-hand, and in the use of your rifle. Your scores are one of the best we have ever had. These will be most useful to you in this assignment. You seem to be very focused when you are in tense situations and I guarantee this will be very tense." The Colonel looked at Tommy as he drew a dark-colored folder from his locked desk drawer. Baskins turned toward Lt. Ransom and said, "What do you think, Lieutenant?"

Ransom looked at Tommy for a few seconds, then returned his eyes to Colonel Baskins and nodded. "It's a go." Then he raised himself from the chair, saluted Colonel Baskins and quietly left the room.

Colonel Baskins stepped out from behind his desk and sat down in the other chair closer to Tommy. He gripped tightly the folder in his hand and said, "We have a very important mission that we are putting together and we would like you to be a part of it."

Tommy leaned forward and said, "I don't understand. What does this have to do with me?"

The Colonel stared at Tommy. "We need someone or a small group of men to get into Tokyo Harbor and take out the mines that are there. We have been watching you for the past two months and we decided that you would be a good candidate. If you accept this assignment, you'll be sent to a camp in Florida for special training. You will be joined by some Marines from other bases in the country. That's all I can say at this time. I need your answer before 1900 today. If you return I will know you have accepted the assignment."

Tommy was in shock. He never thought that he would be chosen for such a mission. What was he missing? What did these people see in him that he couldn't or wouldn't see. He returned to his quarters and lay on his bunk and began to think.

Tommy rolled on his back and slowly opened his eyes. "Holy shit," he hollered, as he jumped from his bunk. He looked at the clock. It was 1830 hours. "I must have fallen asleep. How the hell can I make a decision in an hour?" But he had already made up his mind long before now. He checked himself in the mirror, then headed for Battalion Headquarters. He climbed the stairs two at a time and walked quickly down the corridor toward the Colonel's office. As Tommy approached the desk sergeant, Sergeant Johnson nodded his head and motioned Tommy to go directly into the Colonel's office. He saluted Colonel Baskins and turned toward the other officer in the room. Colonel Baskins introduced him to Captain John Accardi, group leader of the secret mission. Accardi walked toward Tommy and shook his hand. Tommy felt the steel grip of a man who was in combat shape. Accardi was about 6" and weighed 190–200 lbs. He was straight as a 2 x 4 and had a great smile and menacing green eyes. Tommy thought he must be great to be with on the battlefield. Colonel Baskins pointed to a chair next to Capt. Accardi and gestured to Tommy to sit down.

Colonel Baskins sat and looked at the two Marines. "We must move faster than we first thought. We now have only three weeks to prepare. We will begin tomorrow at 0700 here instead of Florida. That's all, gentlemen. We must be up early tomorrow."

Accardi and Tommy left the room and went off in different directions. Tommy paused to light a cigarette, then began to jog toward his room with many thoughts dancing through his head. Where did all of this come from? Where would it end up? Tommy hated surprises.

The bugle sounded at 0530 but Tommy was already awake and dressed. He ran down the stairs and out toward the mess hall. The chow line was short. He selected some scrambled eggs and bacon with dark toast and a cup of coffee, black. He took his tray to a table at the rear of the hall. Quickly he ate his breakfast and got another cup of coffee to enjoy with his cigarette. As he walked outside a jeep pulled to the curb and called his name. Accardi was sitting behind the wheel. He hollered, "Tommy, jump in." Tommy barely had time to climb in the passenger seat when Captain Accardi floored the gas pedal and the jeep roared down the road. It only took seven minutes to get to company headquarters.

They entered the building, talked to the desk sergeant and walked upstairs to the conference room. Two soldiers, fully-armed, were standing at attention at the door. Tommy and Captain Accardi identified themselves by name and serial number. The soldier on the left checked a list attached to a clipboard, looked at the pair and then opened the door.

As they entered the room Tommy saw a large conference table with eleven soldiers sitting at attention. At the end of the table there were two empty chairs. Colonel Baskins rose and motioned them to sit in the end seats. When they were seated Colonel Baskins began speaking. "Good morning, gentlemen. We will hold off on the introductions till later. As you know, we have been planning a mission to help in the invasion of Japan. We have organized you into three teams, one for each target. You won't know your target until twenty four hours before the mission deadline. Open the envelope in front of you. These are the only plans you will see. I want you to read them as a team. Make sure you understand them. Decide who the team leader is. At the close of the session these plans will be collected and destroyed. At 1000 we will board the van and head for the training facility."

Tommy sat with Captain Accardi and two other Marines. To his right was Corporal Sam Pack and Corporal Jim Backman. Both looked to be close to Captain Accardi's age, making Tommy the youngest in the group. Together they huddled around the table and gazed at the envelope. As ranking officer, Captain Accardi took the envelope, broke the seal and took out its contents. On the table he laid a map and one sheet of 8 ½ x 11 typed paper. The map was a detailed drawing of Tokyo Harbor. There were black and red marks drawn on it which indicated possible locations of the mines. The mission was to bring back more precise information about their locations. The sheet of paper detailed the mission as well as a list of supplies and ammunition needed. It also provided information about escape routes. A submarine would be used to get the Marines as close as possible to the harbor. Each group would be dropped at different locations to insure that at least one group reached shore.

Colonel Baskins continued. "The areas we have chosen appear to be the least patrolled but this mission is still very dangerous. Once you land you'll be near villages that our intelligence tells us are more or less safe but you have to be careful. You will do what you have to do to get the information about the mines. You will have 72 hours to complete your mission and meet the sub at the same location where you were dropped off. Make sure you understand the escape routes as listed on the paper in your packet. If you're not there, you'll have a long swim back. The sub won't wait."

The men studied and discussed the information for quite a while before they returned the envelopes to the Colonel. The meeting concluded at 1000 hours. Colonel Baskin escorted the group to a black van that would take the group to the training facility. The side windows of the van were blackened so no one could see outside.

When everyone was seated, the van began its journey. The day was a warm one and the van soon became very uncomfortable, but the windows could not be opened. After about an hour the van came to a halt and everyone piled outside. In front of them was a huge, grey, unmarked building with gigantic doors that curved all the way to the top beyond view. Tommy thought it might be one that could house a large blimp. He remembered the times when some of these airships passed over Boston when he was growing up. There was a similar building to this one in one of the suburbs south of Boston which was used as a blimp hanger.

When they entered they saw that the rear of the building was open and they could see right through to the ocean that was about 300 yards away. Tommy thought it looked bigger than Fenway Park. The side walls which had been made of wood on the outside changed to solid concrete on the inside. Out in the ocean Tommy could see a submarine emerging from the water. It was fascinating to watch but when he thought of the number of hours that he would be spending in that steel contraption; well, he decided not to think about it. After a few minutes one of the lieutenants hollered, "Now we'll show you to your sleeping quarters. After you settle in, go to the mess for dinner. After dinner, we will meet in the conference room at 2000 hours for a brief meeting. Then it will be lights out. We will regroup in the morning."

Tommy could hardly keep his eyes open. He wanted sleep more than he wanted a woman. Well, both would be welcome, but for once he actually preferred the former. Tommy slept very poorly that night but was up for roll call the next morning, ready and eager to begin training. One of the first tasks was to familiarize the group to the environment of a submarine. So, early that morning the 12 marines climbed down the conning tower ladder into the belly of the sub.

Tommy's first thought was how small and narrow it was. He could hardly stand without banging his head. He understood now why none of the marines was over 5'10" tall. When the sub was secured it slowly glided from the dock to the open water. The major goal of today's activity was to expose the marines to submarine life. They would travel about two miles from shore under water, then surface. The marines would run up the ladder and balance themselves on deck as they put air into the large rafts which would take them ashore. Next, the rafts would be lowered into the water and the marines would descend into the rafts and be ready to paddle away from the sub. There would be four marines in each raft; two would paddle while two would stand guard. They would paddle about 200 yards, then return to the submarine. Timing was important. Preparation was important. The results of this insurgence were very important. After an hour at sea the alarm was sounded and the drill began. Tommy's group was the second team up the ladder. When they hit the deck they could feel the rolling of the sea against the sides of the sub. It was difficult to blow up the rafts. Once they were inflated they were tossed over the side and secured with a rope line to the sub. The marines descended a Jacob's ladder, jumping the last few feet into the rafts. Taking their pre-assigned positions they began paddling away from the boat. The water was rough but the marines had the rafts under control. Twenty or twenty-five minutes went by before a horn sounded from the sub, telling the men to turn around and come back. When they were all below deck the submarine descended into the murky water. Colonel Baskins suggested that all the marines meet in the officer's room. He looked a little upset but told the men they had done okay for the first attempt, but they had to improve in all areas for this mission to be a success. He turned the meeting over to Lt. Ransom who went through the whole exercise step by step. The main drawback seemed to be inflating the rafts and getting them into the water. A few suggestions were discussed. It was time for chow.

Tommy joined Accardi and the rest of his team at the end of the mess hall. "What do you think?" he said to the group as he sipped his soda.

"I think we are committing suicide if we don't find another way to get those rafts ready," said Sam Pack with a sly grin on his face.

"I agree," said Jim Backman.

Captain Accardi looked very serious. "I think you're right. What about you, Tommy, what do you think?"

"Well, the way we're doing it now is too slow, especially inflating the rafts, and that makes it more dangerous. If we could figure a way to have the rafts, say, half-inflated, that would help with the problem."

"Yes," answered Accardi, "but how?"

Tommy thought for several seconds, then said, "We can't inflate them in the sub because we would never get them out. But if we can," and here Tommy paused briefly, "half inflate them beforehand and secure them to the deck, it might work." Later, after chow, they brought their idea to Lieutenant Rankins who said he would discuss it with the submarine Captain. By the next morning he would let them know what was decided.

The captain must have liked the idea because as soon as the sun was up the crew and the marines were on deck inflating the rafts and securing them to the side of the sub. Captain Accardi looked at his crew and gave them the thumbs up sign. With smiles on their faces they returned the sign.

After an hour the sub submerged and within twenty minutes the alarm rang again. This time the drill went much smoother and faster. By 1900 hours they had improved so much that the officers called it a day and set sail for port. Probably the next time they would do this it would be for real. The marines had little difficulty falling asleep that night.

The events that took place during the next few days not only cancelled the secret attack but changed the world forever. On August 6, 1945, a silvery, superfortress called the Enola Gay flew over the city of Hiroshima and dropped an atomic bomb. In a single flash of light, followed by a massive fireball, the entire city and its population of 73,000 were disintegrated. Three days later, a similar bomb was dropped on Nagasaki, resulting in thousands more deaths and widespread destruction. On August 10, Hirohito, the Emperor of Japan, accepted the peace treaty conditions which included unconditional surrender. Quickly, the news was transmitted to Colonel Baskins. The Tokyo Harbor operation was no longer necessary.

Within 48 hours Tommy had returned to the United States and begun the mustering out process that relieved him of his military duties. Tommy had mixed feelings about leaving the Marines. He liked the life he was living. He liked the action, the camaraderie, the women, the adrenaline rush that kept him on his toes. If the Tokyo Harbor mission had been successful he would have no doubt risen in rank and probably had more missions just as dangerous offered to him. He had become an important cog in a well run machine. He thought back to his boot camp days, the rigid training and the hand to hand combat where he outclassed everyone else. He loved the feeling of stalking his opponent, sneaking up behind him and thrusting the rubber knife into his heart. It had become a game to him; a game that he excelled at. Little did he realize at the time what a profound change his Marine training would have in his new civilian life.

Just before Thanksgiving, 1945, Tommy Hayes returned to Charlestown. Very little had changed, except him. His brother Norman was working for Mike McCormick, booking numbers. Mike said that there was an opening for Tommy if he wanted it. Tommy felt like taking some time off to think about it. But he didn't want to lose this opportunity, either. He had a funny feeling that this would result in something much larger than just booking numbers.

People in Charlestown noticed the changes in Tommy. He was bigger, stronger looking, his shoulders and arms had really bulked up. He was more confident and outgoing. He talked more and he drank and talked with girls. But it didn't take long for them to see also his anger and his new aggressiveness. It was a Friday night and Tommy and a few friends were drinking in Scalli's Tavern. The regular Friday night fights were on the television. As the night wore on the place got louder. Tommy, Sammy O'Toole, Jim Orpen and Bobby Fitch were standing at the bar throwing down shots and beers and watching the fights. Tony the bartender came over to take the next orders from the group when Sammy hollered down the bar, "Hey, jar head, it's your turn to buy."

Tommy didn't like what he had heard. "What did you say, Sammy?" asked Tommy, as he slowly turned his head to face Sammy.

"I said, 'Hey, jar head, it's your turn to buy.' Did you become deaf while you were sitting on your ass over in the Pacific?" Sammy now had a silly grin on his face.

Nobody else paid attention to what was happening. Tommy slowly inched his way around Jim Orpen and was standing in front of the 6'2" Sammy who had a big smile on his face. Tommy looked him square in the face and said, "I don't like being called a jar head."

Still smiling, Sammy said slowly, pronouncing every word, "But you are a jar head. Isn't it true that once a Marine, or jar head, you are always a Marine or jar head?"

"That's not true," answered Tommy, "and don't call me that again."

He turned and began walking back to his place at the bar when he heard Sammy say, louder this time, "What are you going to do about it, jar head?" All eyes in the bar turned from the television toward Tommy and Sammy.

"Just this," said Tommy as he turned back to Sammy and threw a perfect left jab that broke Sammy's nose. Before Sammy could get his hands up he was hit twice in the stomach and once on his left eye. He grabbed the bar to hold himself up but Tommy moved right in and hit him on the nose again. Blood was pouring out of his nose like water gushing from a fire hose. As Sammy moaned and started to slump to the floor Tommy hit him on the jaw so hard you could hear the bone crack as the blood burst from his mouth along with a few teeth. Everyone backed away as Sammy crumpled to the floor, his face a bloody mess. The patrons were stunned. The carnage had all happened in 10 seconds. Someone hollered to Tony, "You better call an ambulance or this guy is going to die right here."

Tommy moved further up the bar, finished his drink with one swallow and walked out the door without looking back. An observer, one Mike McCormick, sitting in the last booth, looked at his friend and said matter of factly, "He's not going t' be just a bookie much longer." He was right. It wasn't long before Tommy Hayes and Mike McCormick joined forces to become the leaders of the Hayes-McCormick Gang, one of the most feared partnerships in Charlestown.

CHAPTER 7

▼

Jackie thought constantly about Kathleen. He remembered the first night he saw her at the club in the South End. He relived again and again the meeting in the Waldorf. He had been so mesmerized by her eyes. But he didn't know how to approach her. The fact that he wasn't drinking alcohol, which he called a social lubricant, kept him from calling her and asking her for a date. He wanted to in the worst way. Maybe if he just bumped into her in the store he could ask her but this probably would never happen. He didn't even feel like dating other women, so his social life crashed down to practically nothing. There were always a few women at the AA meetings but it was a bad idea to date in AA. He could see the conflicts that it might create. And he was enjoying life, living each day now without a drink. He just wanted in the worst way to meet Katherine again.

Jackie lived in a small, one bedroom, first floor apartment at 27 Pleasant Street in Charlestown. He didn't complain about the $60 a month rent. His landlord, Dennis Flannigan, along with his wife, Lucille, lived upstairs. They were a good Catholic family with, at last count, seven kids, all under the age of 10. Dennis drove a delivery truck for a local company so he was home every night. On Sundays he was one of the collector's at St. Mary's. He wasn't much older than Jackie. He had lived in the house as a kid and inherited it when his mother died a few years ago. Pleasant Street was a typical, residential Charlestown street. It ran from the Bunker Hill Monument at the top of the hill down through some curves to end at the bottom at Warren Street, not too far from historic Warren Tavern, built around the time of the American Revolution. Number 27 was at the bottom.

During the spring and summer months Jackie played baseball in the Boston Park League, one of the oldest amateur leagues in the country. When winter set in he played basketball in the YMCA League in Charlestown.

Between work, AA meetings and sports activities, Jackie's life was fairly full but dull. Different than a lot of jobs, longshoremen had to actually show up and work to get paid. There were no guarantees either. Fringe benefits such as medical insurance or paid holidays and vacation were in their infancy. You had to be at the shape-up locations in order to get hired at least once and sometimes twice a day. Young workers like Jackie who could work down in the ship's hold and produce had an advantage. But you still had to hustle to make a decent week's pay.

Spring was definitely in the air. Heavy winter coats and hats were no longer needed. Flowers were starting to show their heads in garden plots and alongside driveways. You could see the welcome change on people's faces. Neighbors would stop and talk outside with each other. Women could hang their wash out on the line again. Kids were playing baseball in the parks, on the streets or just shouting at one another as they ran around the neighborhood. The mood of the city had changed.

Jackie appreciated the warmer weather just like everyone else. He usually did his food shopping on Thursday evenings but this week he had worked on Thursday so he decided to do it on Saturday afternoon. It was a lovely, sunny day. His favorite store was Sammy's Super Store located on Main Street, not too far from his apartment. As he was turning the corner onto Main Street he caught sight of Kathleen as she was entering the supermarket. Quickly and quietly, he took a carriage and walked up behind her. She wore black slacks and an open blue jacket which revealed a pretty pink sweater. Her trim figure excited Jackie. She looked great. He was excited and nervous at the same time. He had to break the ice somehow. As she turned a corner, she stopped suddenly and Jackie's carriage accidentally hit her back. She jumped and turned with an angry look on her face. When she saw it was Jackie, however, her expression changed and she said, "License and registration, please."

Jackie burst into laughter. "Oh, no, it had to be you. Of all the supermarkets in the world, you had to choose this one."

"Considering it's the only one close to us, it's understandable."

Jackie smiled, tried to relax, and managed to ask, "How are you?"

She said, "Fine, how about you?"

"I'm doing ok."

Jackie began to chew his lip, trying to think of something to say that wouldn't sound stupid.

She stood silent for a few seconds. "Well, I guess I'll finish my shopping." She didn't move, however.

Jackie hesitated, but then asked quickly, almost without thinking about it, "Would you like to get a cup of coffee when you finish?"

She thought for only a second. "Sure. We can meet at the Waldorf, if that's okay with you."

"Great," he answered.

Jackie had never done his shopping so fast. He even neglected to get some things because he didn't want to take the time. Fifteen minutes later they were sitting opposite each other, drinking coffee and eating apple pie a la mode. Years later, they would admit that although this was their first date, they knew it was the beginning of something wonderful, something that they would never forget or regret.

CHAPTER 8

▼

Since that first, impulsive date, Jackie and Kathleen saw each other every chance they could. On one Tuesday evening after they had left each other about 11:00 p.m., Jackie decided to walk down to Chelsea Street to look at the hiring board for the next day. The truth was, he just didn't want to go home yet. He needed to savor the evening that he had just spent with Kathleen. He was on top of the world.

Days were longer now and getting warmer, but it was still cool after the sun went down. As he walked past Doherty's and approached the weeds at the corner of Chelsea and Joyner Streets he looked into the grass and thought he saw something which caused him to stop in his tracks. Could that really be a body in the tall grass? It looked like a person lying on his left side facing the street. Maybe the person was just a drunk, sleeping it off; a not unusual occurrence any night of the week. But then he heard a noise that sounded like crying, like someone was in pain. The body moved slightly. Jackie could just walk away and forget about the whole thing or he could go and see and if the person was actually hurt, not just drunk, then go for help. He walked cautiously down toward the weeds and knelt down on the wet grass so he could get a better look. His heart beat even faster as he stared into the face of Joey Mons. Joey's eyes were glassy as he slowly tried to raise himself up to see who was helping him. When he saw it was Jackie, he tried to speak but no words came out. Slowly, with Jackie helping him, Joey managed to roll over while clutching at his chest. Jackie could see the wound in Joey's body, spurting blood just below his heart. The blood was pouring out like a ruptured water main. Jackie tore off his own jacket and tried to cover the wound with it but the blood continued to flow too fast. Jackie looked again at Joey's face. Joey was trying to tell him something.

"Don't talk, Joey, I've got to get some help," Jackie said, starting to get up.

"No ... no, Jack," Joey managed to say between gasps for air. He grabbed Jackie's arm and pulled him closer. "Get ... out, Jack ... get ... away."

"Who did it, Joey? Who did this to you?"

Joey struggled with his breathing but finally managed between gasps for air to whisper a name. "Paamm, Paammmm," was all he could utter. Blood was now oozing from his mouth. Then, quite calmly, he closed his eyes as his head fell to the side. His body went limp and he became still.

Jackie hesitated a few seconds, then blessed himself before standing up. The name that Joey had whispered to him was repeating itself again and again in Jackie's brain. *Why would anyone kill Joey? Joey was one of the nicest guys around.* Was it robbery, or was there something else that maybe Joey was involved in. Did he really know Joey? *What kind of nightmare have I gotten myself into?* Jackie quickly realized that he had to put these questions on the back burner and figure out what he had to do right now. He heard sounds behind him. Or were they coming from the sidewalk in front of Doherty's? Were they after him now?

His first thought was to go to the police. But first he had to get away from here. Whoever it was could be after him. He stood up and looked once more at Joey. Had anyone seen him go behind the building? He looked all around and saw no one, although he heard voices coming from somewhere. There were a few cars going by but they weren't slowing down. He walked quickly out to Chelsea Street. He stopped before reaching the sidewalk and looked both left and right. He turned right, walking quickly away from the police station, looking every few seconds to see if someone was following him. He rubbed his bloody hands on his already blood-soaked jacket. He rolled this into an even tighter ball and hoped that he didn't have any other visible blood on his clothes which someone could notice.

As he continued up Chelsea Street he noticed a long, black Cadillac parked across the street at the next corner. He could see the outlines of two figures sitting in the front seat. He didn't know if they saw him but he grew increasingly scared as he approached the beginning of the Mystic River Bridge. He crossed the street, half running by the time he got to the other side. At this time of night there wasn't much traffic. He didn't pass anyone on the sidewalk. He glanced over his left shoulder as he headed up Putman Street which led to the Training Field Park. He was sure he wasn't being followed but he didn't dare slow down.

He crossed Park Street into the Training Field Memorial Park. It had been created as a memorial to soldiers who trained there during the Civil War. He was heading toward the area around the Bunker Hill Monument. He had to find a safe place and fast. As he crossed Soley Street he heard the faint sound of a car engine. It seemed to be coming from the next street which was Monument. Thinking quickly, he jogged a little way down Soley Street and stepped into a dark alley. He knew this was dangerous because there was no way out, but he had no choice.

The noise of the car became louder and he pulled his head back into the shadows. All he could do now was hope and pray. He flattened himself against the brick wall of the building. His body was tense but he was ready to run for his life. His athletic training would help him now or he was a dead man. The car turned the corner and was headed down Soley Street. He held his breath and pulled himself tighter to the wall. As the front end of the car cruised slowly by the alley, Jackie relaxed when he recognized a Boston Police cruiser, but then he froze because following not far behind it was the long black Cadillac.

As the sound of the cars drifted away, Jackie thought about what he had to do. Maybe it was just a coincidence that the Cadillac was behind the police cruiser. But he really didn't believe that. There was something mysterious going on and now he was a part of it. He must find some place to hide. He tried to slow down his breathing as he took several deep breaths. He never felt so alone in his life, but he couldn't involve Kathleen. This was a dangerous situation and he didn't want her to get hurt or killed. He knew that there would be empty trucks at the Hoosaic Piers. He could hide there until dawn. It was approaching midnight. He needed to move on before he was spotted. He felt quite confident that he could get to the piers safely by cutting through yards and using alleyways.

After waiting about 10 minutes Jackie walked slowly to the entrance of the alley and peeked around the corner, looking left, then right. It was dark but the street lights were bright enough for him to see in both directions. He took a right and walked confidently up the hill toward the Bunker Hill Monument. As he walked by a dark alley, a set of arms came out to embrace him from behind. Jackie tried to struggle out of his grip.

"Jackie, Jackie, it's me, Dom Sali. I'm not going to hurt you." Jackie stopped struggling and Dom released his arms. Jackie turned around and looked at a familiar face but one that he hadn't seen in a few years. It was Dominic Sali, a guy from the North End whom he played sports with at Charlestown High. The North End didn't have a high school so the North End kids went to Charlestown High. But the face he saw now wasn't the same as he had known as a student. It was hard and cold with eyes that were dark, frightening and piercing. Dom looked into Jackie's eyes and slowly began to speak. Puffs of garlic and cigarette smoke flowed toward Jackie but he didn't flinch. He was afraid that Dom might have a knife or a gun.

Dom, almost in a whisper, said, "The only reason that you're still alive is that I know you. And Carmine don't like what's been happening around here. I'm going to ask you something and I want the truth." Dom moved back a step, then continued. "We saw you go behind Doherty's but we don't know if you saw, well, maybe a body in there. If you did, did he say anything to you? Carmine wants to know."

Jackie thought as quickly as he could. Maybe they didn't see him at the body or know that he actually talked with Joey Mons. He had to pretend—he had to bluff. When Jackie didn't answer, Dom reached up and put a hand around Jackie's throat. The pain was so severe that Jackie was ready to give up and tell him what Joey Mons had said. But at the same time he heard from around the corner the shrill of some prowl cars as they approached. Dom released his grip as he bent over to Jackie and said in a hoarse whisper, "If you say anything, you'll regret it. Or maybe your girl …" Within seconds two black and whites screeched to a stop directly in front of the men.

Two policemen emerged from the cars with billy clubs in hand, ready to bang heads. The leader, a sergeant, hollered as he approached them, "What's going on here?"

Jackie said nothing. It was then that he saw Dom's partner, Coco Cappadonna, who had been hiding in the shadows, step up next to Dom. No one said anything as they waited for the lead officer to get nearer. Again, the cop hollered, "What's going on here? We got a call about a mugging going on at Soley and High Street." He was ready to hit someone if he didn't get an answer quickly.

Jackie figured this was a way for him to get away, so he answered, "Hey, we were just arguing about who was the best player, Ted Williams or Joe DiMaggio. You know, a typical North End, Charlestown argument." Jackie tried to sound convincing, injecting a little laugh as he talked. The sergeant looked very skeptical as he peered intently at the three men. He didn't see any bruises or blood. He shouted while tapping his club against his other hand.

"Get the hell out of here. And if I see you again, you'll be sorry."

Since Jackie had mentioned the North End and Charlestown, Jackie knew that the police would expect them to go in different directions. Dom didn't look Jackie's way as he and Coco walked down Soley Street. The cops returned to their cars. One car followed Dom and Coco down Soley and the other drove slowly behind Jackie, letting him get a head start. After he had gone about 50 yards, Jackie turned around as the prowl car pulled up next to him.

"Get in," said Sergeant Jimmy O'Neil, a former townie whom Jackie knew from the Hayes Square softball league. Jackie got in without hesitation. He kept his bloody hands hidden inside his jacket which he kept rolled up to hide the blood stains. He had held on to it during the whole episode with Dom and Coco. He hoped that he didn't appear as scared as he felt.

"What the fuck was going on there?" shouted O'Neil, glaring at him from the passenger side of the front seat.

Jackie tried to sound convincing as he said, "It really was about a bet we made last week." He had to think fast. "Dom was claiming that I hadn't made the bet that paid $200 because I didn't have a slip. I told him that Bunso Joyce never gave me a slip unless the bet was over $500. I think he was just trying to see if I would cave in."

O'Neil said nothing at first, but only looked directly into Jackie's eyes. Jackie looked directly back at him.

"Okay, get out. Better yet, we'll drop you someplace. We wouldn't want any of your pals to catch up with you again."

"If you get me to the Sullivan Square train station, that'd be great," Jackie managed to say.

The patrol car started up the street for the few blocks and stopped in front of the station. Jackie got out and uttered a weak "Thanks" as he shut the back door. O'Neil just grunted. The patrol car did not move as Jackie walked into the station.

Jackie climbed the stairs to the elevated station, deposited his money in the toll box and walked down the platform. He didn't know what to do or where to go. His head was throbbing, his throat as dry and rough as sand. The platform was empty. Jackie could have sat down on one of the few benches, but he just couldn't force himself to relax. After a few minutes the train approached the station. Its destination was Forest Hills, between Roxbury and Roslindale. Jackie got on board and sat close to the doors, just in case he had to exit fast.

Meanwhile, Dom and Coco walked toward the High Bridge that would take them to the North End. They were half way across the bridge when a black Cadillac pulled beside them. The rear door opened and both got in. Driving the car was Salvatore Casano, a mid-level wise guy and protégé to North End Mob boss, Carmine Mercury. Sitting next to him was Tony-the-Snake Casio, one of the most dangerous strong-men in the mob. He got his nickname because he could slither his way into any locked-up place in town. Maybe it was also because he liked to dress in browns and blacks, sometimes with suit coats that had weird, repetitive patterns. He turned toward the back seat and said to no one in particular "You guys really fucked up." Dom and Coco wisely remained silent. "Now we don't know what the Irish bastard knows. Let's get back to the club and set it up with Carmine. And you two guys better wise up or …" as he quickly slid his hand across his throat.

Jackie rode the train for several hours. He still didn't have a clue to what he was going to do. His options were limited but he had to do something. He crossed to the other side of the platform and stepped onto the train headed toward Everett, with a stop in Charlestown. He certainly didn't want to go to Kathleen's house and jeopardize her safety. He knew that the guys he was dealing with were killers and it would never be a quick death. He tried to sort out the last few hours, from the time that he found Joey Mons' body, until he ended up in the patrol car with Jimmy O'Neil. It didn't make sense. Those guys didn't even know if he saw the body. But then again, maybe they did. And why was Joey killed? He didn't work for the mob or any of the Charlestown gangs, but yet he had been killed gang-land style. It couldn't be a loan sharking debt because those guys might injure you but dead people can't pay. Maybe it was about a woman, but Jackie quickly cast that aside because he knew that Joey didn't fool around. If he did, his wife Maria would have castrated him.

As the train pulled into City Square, Jackie made a decision. He would get off and go to the Armed Service YMCA, located near the train stop. He knew that Roy would be on the desk and would let him in. Jackie had played a lot of basketball at the Y and Roy was a good friend. This was a place where he could hide out for a while. It might even be a good idea to get a room if one was available. Quickly he crossed the street and climbed the stairs and entered the Y. He was relieved when he saw Roy. He would have shaken hands with him but he didn't dare take them from behind his rumbled jacket. He had to get to a bathroom.

"What's up?" yelled Roy, having to speak over the noise of the lobby crowd.

"Nothing much," replied Jackie. "I thought I'd just hang out for a while. Do you have sneakers I can borrow?"

"Sure," answered Roy. "I have lots of them that people leave and never come back for. What size?"

"Ten and a half," answered Jackie.

Roy looked under the counter and came up with a pair of white, high cut Converse All Stars that looked almost new. Roy was going to hand them to Jackie, along with a towel and locker key, but Jackie headed quickly for the locker room, saying he would return in a few minutes. Roy shouted after him "If I get a break I'll challenge you to a game of 21."

"Okay," said Jackie, as he pushed through the locker room door. He looked around and found that he was alone except for a couple of guys at the opposite end of the large room and they were more interested in themselves than anyone else. He sat on a bench near the first row of lockers, clutched his jacket, and looked down at the floor. What a hell of a mess he had gotten himself into, he thought. He carefully unwrapped his jacket a little and looked at the damage. Fortunately, his jacket was dark brown and black, so the blood stains really didn't show too much. He already knew the layout of the room from previous visits so he knew that the toilets and sinks were just around the next row of lockers. His heart was no longer beating like bongo drums and his breathing had calmed down, too. He walked over to the sinks and put the jacket on the floor while he washed his hands. No one paid any attention to him. Then he splashed his sweaty face with warm water and used some paper towels to dry off. Next to him was a large trash barrel, already half filled with used paper towels. He picked up his jacket off the floor, then, along with his own paper towels, stuffed everything into the bottom of the trash bin. Without looking around he exited the locker room. He walked up to Roy who had left the pair of sneakers, as well as a towel and a locker key, on the counter.

"Hey Roy," Jackie called out, "have you got a spare room for a night or two?" As Jackie was signing for the room key, he noticed the small TV which Roy had sitting on his desk. They had just interrupted the main broadcast for a news flash. Both men turned to the TV to listen.

"The body of a man was found this morning behind a tavern in Charlestown. Joseph Mons, 51 years of age, formerly a longshoreman and for many years the bartender at the Eight Bells on Chelsea Street, was found dead of knife wounds by a janitor who was coming to work. Police are asking that anyone with any information to please contact them immediately."

"Hey, Jackie," said Roy, "You come from Charlestown. You know this guy?" As Roy turned to look at Jackie, he found no one there.

Detective Tom O'Malley heard the same news flash at the same time and immediately left his home in neighboring Medford and drove to Station 15 in Charlestown. He called together the rest of his team and within an hour they all were sitting in the detectives' meeting room.

No weapon had been found but they were still looking.

Joey Mons was a likable man who tendered bar at the Eight Bells on Chelsea Street. Joey was described by a few of the patrons who were eager to talk as a friendly guy who cracked Irish jokes once in awhile when things got quiet. He was known to bet a little bit on the numbers and the horses at Suffolk Downs, but nothing extravagant, although he always had an Armstrong newspaper, the Bible of the racing world, on the bar.

Detective O'Malley had given Paulie Castranova the job of looking for information about Mons but this was all he could come up with. Plus, Joey was the kind of bartender who saw nothing, heard nothing, and said nothing. Others added sarcastically that he didn't smell anything either.

Kathleen was getting worried. She thought that Jackie would have called her on Wednesday night. He must have fallen asleep, she told herself. It was 8 a.m. on Thursday and Kathleen was on her way to work. She walked down Green Street heading toward the Thompson Square elevated station. Standing across the street, leaning against a wall and leisurely smoking cigarettes, were Coco Cappadonna and Peter Lyngos. Peter was one of those guys who had the face of an angel and the heart of Satan. Tony-the-Snake had told them to keep their eyes on Kathleen in case he contacted her. They knew how Jackie felt about her and that he would do anything to protect her.

"What should we do now?" asked Coco.

Peter squashed his cigarette butt on the sidewalk and answered, "We wait a minute, then we follow her up the stairs and onto the train. You sit at one end and I'll sit at the other. She gets off at State Street and walks to the Telephone Company. Afterwards, we walk back to the Club and report to Carmine. We do this for a few more days, see what happens."

Kathleen arrived at her job at 8:40 a.m. and sat at her desk to face another day of numbers.

CHAPTER 9

▼

Three days had gone by. Kathleen was very worried. Since they had started dating, Jackie had never gone a day without speaking to her. She had contacted Stevie O'Brien and Paul Murphy, two of Jackie's best friends, but they had not seen nor heard from Jackie for several days. Kathleen knew that Jackie had a few friends on the police force including Sgt. Jimmy O'Neil, but she decided to wait, hoping she would hear from Jackie today. She talked again with Jackie's mother, but she didn't know anything. Kathleen thought that maybe Jackie had started drinking again and was now ashamed to talk with her. She was feeling increasingly uneasy that something was seriously wrong.

Jackie wanted to make contact with Kathleen but was afraid that somehow the mob would find out. How, he didn't know, but still he feared that they would. Who could he get to help him? His friends Stevie and Paul came to mind but they were drinkers and would blab all over the place that they had heard from him.

At the Italian Social Club in the North End, there were private meetings taking place. Tony-the-Snake was at the head of the table. Tony was a very strange guy. His parents had arrived from Sicily during the early 1900's. They lived in Quincy for a while in a small, two room apartment in the Finnish/Swedish part of the city near Brewer's Corner. His father was an experienced stonecutter and easily got employment in the Quincy quarries. In those days the various nationalities, whether they were Italians, Irish, Finns or Swedes, seemed to get along with each other, even if they did keep within their own ethnic group. After a few years, when some of their neighbors from their home town in Sicily settled in the North End, Tony's family decided to move there too.

Also at the Club was Joey Vigatano. Joey V. was born in the North End in 1914. He was baptized at St. Leonard's Church and lived quietly on Salem Street for many years. He attended St. Leonard's grammar school but when he was 13 he had to leave and find a job because the family was very poor. That's when his life began to change.

There was a lot of small time gambling going on in the North End; craps, blackjack and coin pitching were among the more popular games. Teenagers who were selected by the gang that belonged to the North End Social Club were running them. Joey V., at some point, started hanging around with Fatso Gallante, whose brother was one of the teenage leaders. At first, Joey just watched. But very quickly he became absorbed with the action and wanted to be a player. Fatso wasn't really fat at all but had been called this by his father who really was, tipping the scales at 270 pounds. Fatso showed Joey how to switch dice without being noticed. Joey learned fast but that wasn't what he really wanted to do. Blackjack was his game. He waited patiently and one night, in August, Fatso's brother, Angelo, called him aside and said that it was about time Joey learned to play blackjack and learn how to cheat while playing it. Joey was a fast learner and soon became the teacher. From that point on, no one who knew him would ever play against him.

The head of the North End Mob was Carmine Mercury. He was born and raised in the North End. He had been arrested many times but was found guilty only once. That was for bookmaking because he wasn't fast enough to get rid of the slips. He did six months in the county lockup. That was when he was 21 years old. While he was in jail he was requested to take out another prisoner, Jeddy Rooter, who was considered to be a stool pigeon, thus a liability. Carmine's resourcefulness surprised the mob's upper echelon. He was able to kill, and even dispose of the body, very quickly. Jeddy was never found. When Carmine was released from jail he immediately joined the local mob. He blazed a path of crime and brutality that was unheard of in the New England area. Within five years he was a key mob figure and, as predicted, became a mob boss in 1952.

The Hayes-McCormick Gang took care of its own in Charlestown and Somerville, paying a gratuity to the North End Mob each month. This was to avoid a blood bath between the two groups. They tolerated each other and kept within their restrictive boundaries. Neither one liked to have any notoriety, especially anything which attracted the police, although each gang had its own inside information and informers. The North End Mob was the older, larger and stronger of the two, being able to reach out to gangs in New York and Providence for additional foot soldiers.

The drug scene was moving quickly from New York City to New England, especially to the large cities like Boston, Worcester, Providence, Portland and Nashua. The main supply traveled from New York City to the major cities and then was distributed to local towns and neighborhoods. Then it was put in the hands of neighborhood gang leaders. These people knew the drug addicts and what their drug of choice was. There were payoffs made to local city and state authorities, including the police. Most people thought that this was a fad and would soon blow over. How wrong they were.

Carmine had dealers working in every section of Boston. He had small time leg breakers watching them and his strong arm goon squad, headed by Tony-the-Snake, oversaw the whole operation. The profits were tremendous. There wasn't much work to it either, especially for the higher ups. Carmine ran the operation with an iron fist. People who screwed up were brutalized in such a way that they wished they were dead.

Tony-the-Snake and Carmine worked well together. Tony was very quiet and could move about without being noticed. On the other hand, everyone knew when Carmine entered the room. He was 6'2" and had been pumping iron since he was 16. He had a voice that could shatter windows and a fist that could destroy someone's face with one blow. But those who knew him well loved him. He took good care of his friends. Carmine also had a rather unique advantage over any other person in the local mob. He had had trouble over the years with his eyes which required him to wear large, thick glasses. What you saw more than anything else when you looked at him were two black, sinister ovals surrounding thick, coke-bottle lenses. Black, bushy eyebrows extended out over the tops of the rims. He was one, intimidating guy.

Carmine and Tony were very upset with the killing of Joey Mons. If Joey had told Jackie anything, anything at all, especially if it pointed to one of his own guys, then Carmine wanted to know. The meeting at the North End Social Club was just beginning. Carmine started the conversation. "We don't know who killed Joey Mons or why." Emphasizing his words by wrapping his knuckles on his desk and looking directly for a few seconds at each one in the room, he continued. "But we can't afford de heat. Even if somebody in Hayes' Gang did it, de cops will still want to snoop around here. We have t' find Jackie Monyhan, fast, t' see what he knows."

Tony-the-Snake jumped in. "We're watching all his friends so he can't make a move without us knowing."

"Well, he wouldn't leave wid out his girlfriend. What do we know about her?" barked Carmine.

Coco and Peter had entered the room a few minutes before and now looked at each other to see who should talk first. Coco spoke first. "She works for New England Tele and is a great looker. They say that Jackie sobered up after he met her."

Peter added, "So far, she just goes to work and comes right back home."

"Keep a tail on her. He's bound t' contact her or set up a place to meet," said Carmine. "We all know why Charlie and Pooch were killed. We told them, 'Don't use drugs.' They paid the price because they were stupid. The cops will never figure it out. We got them before they could set us up and now others will know the consequences if they try t' do the same thing. But this Joey Mons thing needs to be wrapped up. I don't want any heat."

Out in Medford, Joey Mons' wake was held at Vincent's Funeral Home. Joey's parents were still living, so the funeral was old fashioned with lots of family and friends in black attire. The younger generation wore black veils to pay homage to their elders. As always, the guys from Charlestown, which included longshore-men, freight handlers, truck drivers, several lawyers, businessmen and a few politicians, were gathered together in the smoking lounge. Although the Eight Bells was considered a dive, its customers considered Joey a friend and a gentleman. Many of them had been helped by Joey when times were tough. Joey never expected anything in return, except maybe a donation to a fund which customers could contribute to. When the fund built up, Joey would donate it to help someone in the neighborhood. The smoke and conversation in the lounge was as thick as a dense fog in mid-Atlantic. The major topics for discussion were: who killed Joey, where was Jackie Monyhan, were the two connected, and, if they were, how?

Detectives O'Malley and Castranova were at the wake to see if they could get any information. Look, listen and process was the motto of Detective O'Malley. His whole team felt the same way. They pooled their strengths to offset their weaknesses, working like a well-oiled machine.

The room became quiet as Mike McCormick walked toward the head of the room and knelt in front of the casket. He blessed himself, his whiskey soaked voice saying, "In the name of da father, an da son, an da Holy Ghost, ahmen." In his rude, arrogant manner he muttered loud enough for all to hear, "We'll get da bastard wud did this; we luv'd ya."

He rose and hugged Joey's widow and children and then walked to the lounge and shook hands with all the Charlestown guys. Some, he looked squarely in the face, while others he just ignored, gazing over their shoulders as he quickly shook their hands. As he walked toward the chairs in the corner, the men sitting there rose and found other chairs. Most knew that Mike wouldn't stay long, especially after he saw the two detectives. Everyone assumed that there would be many plain-clothes cops in the crowded room. As Father O'Malley entered to say the traditional rosary, Mike and his bodyguard left the room. Nobody really cared; everyone was relieved.

After the rosary had been given, the room was very quiet. The door opened and Tommy Hayes walked in. He looked straight ahead, acknowledging no one. He approached the casket, looked briefly at Joey, knelt down on the kneeler, crossed himself and uttered a silent prayer. His eyes came up to look again at Joey. Tommy stood up, turned and found Joey's wife sitting on a chair close to the casket. He extended his hand and she gently accepted it. No words were spoken. Tommy nodded to other members of the family, turned and left the room. No one said anything for a few seconds. Slowly, conversations resumed to their previous level.

Jackie had remained in his room at the Y for the entire three days, only venturing out late at night to grab a pizza and coke at the Pizza Garden, located nearby. But he decided that he had to leave the Y and get a message to Kathleen. If he could get a change of clothes or take on a disguise, he would try it. He went to the end of the locker room where they deposited old clothes to see if he could find something suitable. He looked through a basket filled with old sweat socks, jockstraps, t-shirts, underwear and shorts. Slowly he walked toward the area where he saw something that appeared to be another locker room. There was a dirt-covered sign that read "Military Personnel Only." This was left over from the war days when the building was an Armed Services YMCA. Most of the lockers were damaged and some of the doors were ripped from their hinges. Jackie saw something in one of them that looked like a sailor uniform. Even though the war had been over for years, there were still naval ships docked at the Charlestown Navy Yard. He ripped the suit out of the locker and held it up to his 6' frame. It was a little big but that was better than being too small. He took off his clothes and tried on the suit. It was dirty and stained, but the fit wasn't bad. If he ran into people, he could fake being drunk and pull the sailor hat over his eyes and stagger. He knew how to do that; he had had plenty of practice. He decided to wait until it was dark before he ventured outside. He had to get from the Y at City Square along

Rutherford Avenue or Main Street to reach Kathleen's apartment on Austin Street which was located close to Thompson Square.

It was two o'clock when Jackie went out the side door of the Y. He was facing the low bridge. He turned so he was looking at Station 15, located on the other side of City Square. Staggering a bit he walked along Rutherford Avenue past Joe's Pizza Bar. He followed this route until he came to Austin Street. As he turned the corner he scanned the cars that lined the street. He saw a parked car that looked familiar, about a half a block down on the other side of the street. It was a long black Cadillac, similar to the one that Dom was in last night. If it were the same car it meant that his problem had become more serious, that they knew where Kathleen lived and had been watching her. He saw cigarette smoke coming out from both side windows, which told him that there were at least two in the car.

Inside the car Dom was killing time by telling Coco how he had won three hundred dollars at Wonderland Dog Track. As he was talking, he noticed the sailor coming around the corner. Coco also saw him.

"Ah, it's some poor guy, trying to get back to his ship," concluded Dom.

"Yeah, good luck on getting back before somebody rolls him," replied Coco with a laugh.

Jackie knew he had to get to Kathleen's apartment and warn her, but how? She lived on the first floor. He also knew that there was a back entrance off the alley between the two buildings. Maybe the mob guys didn't know this and wouldn't have it covered. He staggered slightly as he wheeled back around the corner, looking for the alley. He wandered in as if he was going to pee. There was a gate in front of the rear entrance and it was open. He paused and looked around quickly before he entered the yard. Cautiously, he turned the handle on her apartment door and pulled it toward him. He decided to quietly call her name, hoping that she would recognize his voice and not be frightened by someone coming through the back door.

"Hello, Kathleen, it's handsome Jack." The house remained silent. Jackie called again but still there was no answer. He tiptoed through the kitchen into the parlor. He studied the room to see if anything was out of the ordinary. Next to the box where she kept letters and stationary he saw a large envelope with his name written on it. Under his name was written, "EMERGENCY." Jackie ripped open the envelope. A piece of writing paper fell to the floor. Quickly Jackie scooped up the letter and began to read. It was in Kathleen's unmistakable handwriting.

Jackie—

Jimmy O'Neil found out Carmine is looking for you.—he said something's strange going on with Charlestown and North End mobs. He wants me to go with him to see Carmine. Suspicious car been out front. Went out back way. Will meet you at our favorite place later. Meet me there. Luv you—K

Go with him to see Carmine? Jackie didn't like the sound of that at all. What did they want with Kathleen. *This is crazy!*

Jackie knew exactly where she wanted to meet him. But first he had to get out of the house without anyone seeing him. He went upstairs to look out the window to see if the car was still there. Yes, it was in the same spot. He returned to the back of the apartment and went out the same door he had come in. He closed the back gate and walked slowly to the corner. He decided he had to walk away from the building, back the way he had come, even if it looked suspicious. Once he had gotten around the next corner, he could double back another way to return to the Y.

Dom and Coco were still sitting in the car, bored and almost falling asleep. Coco was the first to see the drunk in the sailor suit again.

"There's that sailor again. What's he doing? Did you see where he went before?"

Dom straightened up in his seat and stared down to where Jackie had just come around the corner from the back of the house.

"Where's anybody goin' to get a sailor suit unless they're really in the Navy? Relax. The guy probably just went for a pee."

"Yeah," answered Coco. He checked his watch. "It's almost time for Pete and Jocko to take over. I'm starved. Let's get something at Dunkin' Donuts before we head back to the Club."

Jackie got back to the Y safely, went directly to his room and changed back into his regular clothes. He was somewhat relieved that the police were now involved. He had no doubt that Jimmy O'Neil would stay with Kathleen and provide protection. He had to end this thing fast, though. Perhaps the best thing to do was to turn himself in to Jimmy and let the police solve the mystery. But what was the mystery? All he knew was that after he had discovered Joey Mons' body crazy things had started to happen.

Dom and Coco walked casually into the Club, drinking the last of their Dunkin' Donuts coffee. There were a few customers at the bar and at the tables against the wall. The bosses were probably in the back room. Slowly they walked toward the door to the back room. Dom turned the knob and pushed the door open. Startled, Dom and Coco looked into the faces of Kathleen and Boston Police Sergeant Jimmy O'Neil. Carmine waved his finger and pointed, motioning for them to sit. Dom started shaking. He didn't see any weapons. What on earth were they doing here?

Carmine looked at them and made no attempt to conceal his disgust. "You two could fuck up a high mass." Dom didn't even blink an eye. He knew that he had to take the verbal attack without showing any emotion. But he was grinding his toes through the soles of his shoes.

"What a pair of screw ups," Carmine shouted at them. "You couldn't even keep track of a fuckin' broad, especially one that would stand out in a room full of movie stars."

Kathleen blushed, but stared straight ahead. This was the advice that Sgt. O'Neil had impressed upon her before they had entered the room: Don't talk unless spoken to. Don't smile or laugh. Even though we're here voluntarily, so to speak, anything can happen. I'll have to give up my revolver, but I'll have no choice and Carmine's word is usually good. Just don't do anything to aggravate him.

Jackie had arrived at the location Kathleen had written in her note but she was nowhere to be seen. Maybe Sergeant O'Neil had taken her to a safe place and he shouldn't worry so much. But he wasn't sure of anything, anymore. *What should I do now? Where should I go?*

At the North End meeting, Carmine made it clear that he was in charge. He continued to glance in disgust at Dom and Coco as if they were lower than dog shit. They just tried to avoid Carmine's eyes, while bouncing back and forth on their toes. Carmine barked loudly as he tapped his fingers of his right hand on the table and glanced around at everyone. "Remember, everything said in this room stays in this room or the consequences could be ..." He raised his arms in the air and shrugged his shoulders. The other participants looked at each other and nodded their heads in agreement.

Kathleen was shaking. Sgt. O'Neil touched her hand, trying to calm her down.

Carmine continued. "What we're here for is t' find out what happened t' Joey Mons and what Jackie Monyhan knows about it. Now, don't jump on your high horses. I'm not accusin' anyone of anything. But Jackie was there. So, let's find him and ask."

Sgt. O'Neil looked at Carmine after which Carmine pointed his meaty finger at him and said, "Personally, I don't think Jackie had anything to do wid it, okay? He and Joey were good friends, I know." Then Carmine smiled and added sarcastically with a sickening smile, "But sometimes … best of friends hurt each other. It's part of business."

"But Jackie wasn't in the business," said Kathleen.

Carmine stared at her, leaned forward in his chair and shouted, "You talk when I ask you to talk!"

Sgt. O'Neil clutched at Kathleen's arm and glared at Carmine saying, "She doesn't know the rules."

Carmine glared back and quietly and emphatically said, "Then teach her." He waived his arms in the air as he rose from his chair and growled, "Enough, enough, let's put this away or we'll get no place. Does anyone have any idea where Monyhan is? I promise you, on my mother's soul, that nothing will happen t' him."

Kathleen looked at Sgt. O'Neil, then Carmine, and shook her head no.

O'Neil in turn looked at Carmine and said, "I haven't seen Jackie since I dropped him at the Sullivan Square station." Neither Jimmy nor Kathleen mentioned the note she had left for Jackie.

Carmine had a very frustrated look on his face as he heard a knock on the door. The door slowly opened and Rudy-the-Tank Romboli peeked in, holding a note in his pudgy hand.

Carmine waved him in. "This better be good." He grabbed the note from Rudy's hand and pointed to the door. Rudy didn't hesitate to exit. Carmine adjusted his glasses and looked at the note. The expression on his face didn't change except for a slight nod. He pointed a finger at one of the goonies. "Tank, take Dom and Coco out to the bar and buy them a few drinks—strong ones. We'll have to think of something they can do that's easy and doesn't require too much thinking. Like maybe shovel horse shit against the tide." Once they had left the room he said, "Okay, okay. Very interesting." He leaned forward in his chair and spoke directly to Kathleen, speaking slowly and pronouncing each syllable. "So, my pretty lady, if you talk with your boyfriend Jackie, that is, talk to him before I do, tell him he's off de hook. I don't need to talk wid him." He stopped, then added with a grin, "He's lucky we have some mutual friends."

Kathleen and Sgt. O'Neil looked surprised at each other but said nothing.

While ripping up the note he turned to stare at Sgt. O'Neil and with an edge to his voice added, "And maybe you, Mr. Policeman, if you want to solve this case, maybe you should look a little closer at someone in Tommy Hayes' Gang." At that, Carmine waved one hand in the air, which was the signal for Kathleen and Sgt. O'Neil to leave. After they had gone, Carmine picked up the phone and dialed a number from memory.

"Hey … Ya, it's me. I just got your note. Tell me what goes on here."

CHAPTER 10

▼

On the steps outside the Italian Social Club, Sgt. O'Neil and Kathleen stopped, both breathing a sigh of relief. "That wasn't very nice," he whispered to Kathleen.

"I'm glad that's over. I'm sorry I said something that I shouldn't have. Now what? What could have been in that note?"

"Good question." They both started walking quickly down the street, heading for the car. Sgt. O'Neil took Kathleen by the arm. "I'd love to know what was in that note and who sent it. But for now, we still have to find Jackie and tell him that Carmine isn't looking for him anymore. And he still has to answer some questions for me, like just what does he know about Joey Mons. And what did Carmine mean about looking for someone in Tommy Hayes' Gang?"

Kathleen quickly replied, "You don't think, then, that Jackie had anything to do with Joey's murder?"

"No, but I still have to get some answers," said O'Neil.

Kathleen thought for a few seconds and said, "If he got my note at the apartment, he would have gone to the Old Cemetery Training Field on Bunker Hill Street. When I didn't meet him there he might have left something, to let me know where he'd be."

They got into the unmarked police car and slowly wound their way out of the narrow streets of the North End. Traffic was always heavy. O'Neil turned right at the High Bridge and sped up as he entered City Square. He pulled up in front of Station 15 and left the car running. As he jumped out he called back to her, "I just have to check in. Be right back." He went to the front desk and asked the man on duty to call Captain Nolan and tell him that O'Neil was back but had to go out again on the same case. O'Neil turned and hustled out the door. He jumped into the car, threw the car in drive and pulled out into the traffic.

Kathleen touched his sleeve and said, "Go to the Training Field and I'll check the place where I told Jackie to meet me." O'Neil turned up Warren Street and then up Park to get to the Training Field. It was beginning to get dark; the street lights were starting to come on. As they reached the middle of the field, Kathleen told him to slow down, then said, "Stop here." As she opened the door she hesitated, looking both ways as if she might have been followed.

O'Neil smiled and said, "Don't worry, I've been checking. We're in the clear. Besides, the North End Mob is no longer interested. They take care of their loose ends very quickly."

Kathleen stepped from the car and walked toward the entrance. She turned right and walked into the park. When she passed the second bench, the one that had become their favorite, she stopped and looked around. No one else was in the park. After several seconds of just looking at the bench, she knelt down and looked underneath. She ran her hand under the wooden seat, found something, then pulled it down. She stood up and ran back to the car. She closed the door and opened her hand. In the center of her hand was a ticket stub for the Hippy, the Thompson Square Theater. She pulled off the gum that had held it to the bench. She looked at the ticket and, almost with a happy smile on her face said, "He wants me to meet him at the movies."

O'Neil grinned, saying, "How did you figure that out?"

Kathleen replied, "We saw some spies do it like that in a movie we saw last month and we both mentioned how clever it was. I just guessed he would remember to do it now."

It was nearly 7:30 p.m. when Jackie staggered down Main Street, approaching Thompson Square Movie Theater. In Charlestown, drunks didn't stand out. He didn't know who he could trust so he trusted no one. He hoped that Kathleen would look for the ticket he had left under the bench. If she had found it, she would be at the movie tonight. He approached the ticket window, bought a ticket then went directly to the concession stand and bought a Hershey bar and a bag of popcorn like other movie goers. As he walked through the entrance into the blackened theater he turned right and sat in the last row against the back wall. This was called the necking row when he was a kid. He opened the popcorn as the lights dimmed and the previews began.

Kathleen had taken a quick shower and changed her clothes and was getting ready to leave the house when the phone rang. She lifted the receiver and heard the voice of Sgt. O'Neil.

"I'm off duty now. I'll pick you up in a few minutes and drive you to the movie. After you go in, I'll drive around the neighborhood and double back to see if anybody is hanging around. I'll park, double park if I have to, just down the street from the theater."

Kathleen said okay and waited nervously for him to pull up out in front of the apartment. She tried to calm herself down, telling herself that O'Neil would be there to help her and Jackie if there was any trouble.

Five minutes later O'Neil arrived. She ran down the front steps and into his car. They headed toward Thompson Square. Neither one said a word. A few minutes later O'Neil stopped the car in front of the Alibi Club. He turned to Kathleen and looked her in the eyes. "Remember, I'll be just down the street."

They looked silently at each other, each giving the other a quick, nervous smile. She looked all around, then opened the door and got out of the car, crossed Main Street and headed for the entrance to the movie theater. O'Neil pulled into traffic, took a left and drove up Wood Street. He drove one block and turned right onto Green Street, passed the Boy's Club, then turned right to return to Main Street where he parked close to the Pilsen Gardens Bar. He could see the movie theater through his rear view mirror.

As Kathleen bought her ticket she was both anxious and excited. She couldn't wait to see Jackie if he was there. Oh God, she prayed, let him be there. When she entered the darkened theatre she noticed that the main feature had already started. She waited a few seconds until her eyes had adjusted. She then ventured into the dark, slowly advancing toward the last row in the back. There were a lot of empty seats and those that were taken were scattered throughout. Suddenly, a hand reached out and gripped hers tightly and drew her into the aisle seat.

"Kathleen, it's me, Jackie," he whispered. "Are you okay?"

She turned and fell into his arms and crushed her lips against his. For a few seconds they hugged fiercely, then let each other go.

"Did anyone follow you?" he asked quickly in a hoarse whisper.

"No, no, don't worry," said Kathleen. "Sgt. O'Neil is outside. You don't have to worry, Carmine isn't looking for you any more. They know you didn't have anything to do with Joey Mons' murder."

"What do you mean? How do you know anything about that?"

"Let's go outside, see O'Neil. He'll explain everything. He just needs to ask you some questions."

Jackie hesitated, but Kathleen was determined to lead him out of the theater. They held hands as they headed outside toward O'Neil's car. O'Neil jumped out and came running back to them.

"Boy, am I glad you're okay. And you can relax, there a just a few questions I need to ask, but they can wait until tomorrow. In the meantime, Kathleen can fill you in. Jump in, I'll give you a ride home."

Jackie looked at Kathleen and smiled, then said, "If it's okay with you, I think we'll walk; maybe stop at Joe's Bar and Grill for a pizza."

Kathleen gave a nod of agreement and they grabbed for each other's hands. Jackie then looked O'Neil directly into his eyes when he added, "Thanks for all you've done. We'll never forget it. And after this is all over, we want to keep in touch."

O'Neil got back into his car as Jackie and Kathleen stepped away from the curb. "That's okay, you just owe me big time, pal," O'Neil yelled through the open window as he started to pull away.

CHAPTER 11

▼

Jackie continued to work on the waterfront. But he was having second thoughts about being a longshoreman for the rest of his life. Longshoring was physically demanding with unpredictable hours that resulted in an unreliable paycheck every week. Physically, he was up to working the hours, and the money was good, but the fluctuating paycheck was increasingly worrisome. The chance for accidents and permanent injuries didn't really upset him. Hell, he said to himself, I could get killed just crossing City Square, the way people are driving. Working outside in all kinds of weather started to bother him more. Whether it was the biting cold in the winters or the dripping hot in the humid summers, he was realizing that the job was just a job and not a profession with any real hope for advancement. After many discussions with Kathleen, he came to realize that he didn't want to be a longshoreman for the rest of his life.

During the year following the Joey Mons' murder he and Kathleen had married. Thanks to his friendship and many conversations with Sgt. O'Neil following Joey Mons' murder, he found himself becoming more interested in law enforcement. He even started to seriously consider a profession in police work, but couldn't make himself do anything about it. It was on an early November day in 1953, however, that helped decide Jackie's fate.

It was a lovely fall day, Monday, November 2, 1953. Work had been plentiful for several days with crews working on ships all around the city. Today, Jackie was working on a lumber ship that had docked at Castle Island in South Boston, directly opposite to berth nine at the Boston Army Base. He was working with his partner Art Spector, a young apprentice and a Southie native. It was early afternoon, just after they had returned from lunch. They were on the boat deck, making up a load of 2 x 4's when they heard the first explosion, followed quickly by several others.

"Holy shit," exclaimed Art, as they both immediately dropped the wood they were holding. "What the hell was that?" The noise had come from across the water.

Both men turned around to face the ship being unloaded at the Army Base, the Norwegian freighter, the Black Falcon. Flames were shooting out of hold number four like they were coming from a flame thrower.

"Oh, my God," said Jackie. "That's Mike Sullivan's job."

Explosions were coming one after another now, booming across the water and showering the Black Falcon, water and adjacent pier with charred debris. All work on the lumber ship stopped as everyone came rushing on deck. They could see men trying to get out of the hold of the Black Falcon, but the intense heat forced them back. Another explosion was heard and more flames leapt out of the hatch.

"Let's get over there and see if there's anything we can do," yelled Jackie. Without another word he and Art hurried down from the ship and climbed into Jackie's car which was in a nearby parking lot.

"What the hell was she carrying?" asked Art.

Jackie started the car, put the car in gear, jammed down on the accelerator, not letting up until they reached the intersection where the lot met L Street. He looked quickly to his left. No one was coming. He jerked the car to the right and accelerated down the street.

"There were all kinds of things on it but I know there was bauxite. I was going to work on it, but it came in on a Sunday, so they got the non-union guys to take it."

They could hear more explosions.

"What's bauxite?" asked Art.

"It's used in making aluminum. Kind of tricky stuff. You have to shovel it out. Maybe somebody lit a cigarette. And I think it also had sodium peroxide. It can't stand any kind of heat. I don't know," he added in desperation. "Maybe you can't get it wet either. Things can happen so fast."

Jackie soon caught up with other cars heading in the same direction. He had to slow down to a crawl as both strained to look into the distance.

"Damn, we won't be able to drive much further."

"And it's only going to get worse."

Jackie pulled over to the curb at the first open space he saw and parked. Both jumped out and began running toward the Army Base entrance. When they reached the Edison plant the flaming ship came into full view.

"Jesus," said Jackie. "It's even worse that I thought." Smoke and flames covered the stern of the ship. The forward end was not burning but it was covered with debris.

"Jesus, look how high the flames are. They're reaching the tops of the booms." Two tugs approached the ship.

"What are they going to do?" called Art over to Jackie.

"Maybe they're going to try and move the ship away from the pier," said Jackie. Both men were sweating and breathing hard now from running.

The scene at the main entrance was chaotic. A few police who worked along the waterfront were already stationed there, allowing only emergency vehicles and officials through. Police, fire trucks and ambulances were streaming in, one after the other. More sirens could be heard in the distance. Jackie and Art slowed down and tried to find someone they knew. Jackie spotted Kenney McCluske, a cop from Charlestown, as they approached the main entrance.

"Kenney," Jackie yelled but his voice was lost in the noise. He yelled louder, "Hey, Kenney, over here!"

Kenney finally saw the two familiar longshoremen and ran over to them. He was also out of breath, his face having turned a crimson red. The three were in a close huddle now, facing the burning ship, straining to hear each other over the noise.

"Jackie. Thank God you weren't working on this one today."

"Yeah," answered Jackie. "Someone was looking out for me. What have you heard? Do you know much yet? What set it off?"

"Don't know much yet. I was just coming back from a break. It started in the number four hold. First reports say that there were 21 men trapped down there."

The scene was a frenzy of confusion with firemen, police and other emergency personnel running with equipment, trying to get closer to the Black Falcon. Fire hoses were quickly being stretched out all over the dock, each one soon engorged to capacity and spitting out water toward hold number four and all around the deck and pier. Ladders were soon propped up leading from the pier to the ship's rail. Each one had a fireman balanced on one of the top rungs, holding a hose and directing water into the hold.

Several times it looked like the flames had died down, only to erupt again after another explosion. Thick, black, noxious smoke billowed all over the ship and down over the adjacent pier. As they stared at the ship, they saw a man emerging from the hold, his hand grabbing at the coat of another beneath him as they both struggled onto the deck at the mouth of hold number four. Once onto the deck, the first man's hair and clothes suddenly burst into flames. Others yelled to him as he started slapping at his clothes. He fell down, then got up and staggered toward the side before tumbling into the water between the ship and the pier. Some men from the pier jumped in after him.

More ambulances and police arrived. Jackie and all the other longshoremen who had run to the scene couldn't do anything but watch, feeling devastated and painfully useless. Groups of longshoremen huddled together, unable to move, their eyes moving back and forth between the deck of the ship and the men working desperately on the pier. Wives and children of those longshoremen who were working on the ship tried to get through but the police kept them back. Thousands of spectators lined the streets and chain-link fences, every head riveted onto the nightmare that was playing out in front of them. The smoke and soot got worse as the flames died down, forcing the spectators to move back.

The flames were contained after another hour, but there was still heavy smoke pouring out of the hold. Emergency personnel were now able to get onto the ship. Stretchers were soon taking bodies off. Ambulances started to leave the scene, sirens screaming, headed for Boston City Hospital or the Carney in Southie.

After another hour, Jackie had had enough. He and Art started walking back to the car, their mood somber. Often they turned around to look back to the Black Falcon, the ship acting like a magnet that didn't want to let them go. Once in the car, Jackie quickly started the engine and made a U-turn. Neither one spoke as they headed up L Street. Jackie broke the silence and said without emotion, "Let's stop at Saint Mary's and say a prayer." Art agreed with a silent nod.

Jackie never forgot that day and how close he had come to being one of the seven longshoremen who were killed, or one of the many who were severely injured or permanently disabled.

During the next year Jackie filled out the paper work to take the civil service exams for the police and fire departments. He scored high on both exams but there were a number of veterans who got placed higher on the list. He was number 15 on a list of 50. Fortunately, the police department took 18 recruits. He passed the physical exam with ease and entered the Police Academy on September 1, 1957. Like most things, Jackie worked hard, followed instructions and didn't complain. After six months he graduated from the Academy with high honors and was stationed at the South End Division, directing traffic. He was assigned the intersection of Washington and Massachusetts Avenue, one of the busiest intersections in the city. Kathleen would remark how spiffy he looked in his uniform, especially with the white gloves which traffic officers wore. He stopped working full time on the docks, but continued to pay his longshoreman's union dues to Local 799, knowing that he could always earn extra pay on his days off.

Although police work could be a boring job, Jackie made up his mind right from the beginning to make it more interesting. He tried to make friends with some of the neighbors as he and a partner walked their beat in the South End, near the Northampton Station which was part of the Orange Line of the Boston subway system. The Orange Line was a big, ugly overhead structure that took people from the South End to the center of Boston. It had been built at the turn of the century. The politicians had threatened to tear it down, but it remained an eyesore for many more years. Jackie knew that if he did his job well here, he would be moved to a patrol area in due time.

When the morning rush hours were over, he patrolled the stretch of Washington Street which ran from Northampton Station to the Dover Street Station. Then he would cut down to Columbus Avenue which ran parallel to Washington Street. He would return to traffic duty at 12 noon. The district was a cosmopolitan of nationalities. There was a large number of Irish families who attended Cathedral Church schools. There were also Armenians, Lithuanians, Italians, Portuguese and a growing number of black families, many of whom had recently migrated from the south.

But the biggest problem in the area wasn't the various nationalities but the habitual winos, or the occasional drunks, or the prostitutes who walked the streets mostly at night. The winos and the drunks caused problems by bothering people for money or doing just about anything to get themselves a drink. They also prowled the bars early in the morning to get that "eye opener", a drink which would relieve them of the shakes, maybe even a swallow of bread to set their stomachs straight. If they couldn't get some alcohol into their systems, they might experience a seizure or the DT's and end up in the emergency ward or the county lock-up where they would dry out for a day. Jackie discovered quickly that the best way to handle them was to just keep them on the move. Some officers would push them behind a building and beat them up. Ironically, it seemed that the same policemen would often end up drunk themselves after finishing their tours. Other officers would buy a bottle of cheap port wine so the winos could share it and not get sick. Jackie did neither. He just tried to keep them moving, to keep them from interfering with people who were just walking down the street.

Jackie's big chance to prove himself came about a year and a half later. He was patrolling the streets on a late October afternoon near the First National Bank on Washington Street opposite to the Northampton Station. As he approached the bank he noticed a car with its engine running, with the man behind the wheel appearing nervous and looking all around every few seconds. Jackie casually walked up and down the street, trying to decide whether this was just a harried commuter waiting for someone to come down from the train station or perhaps someone who was waiting for some friends to exit the bank. He didn't want to take too much time to answer his own questions. He saw a police call box located about 20 feet beyond the bank entrance. He walked indifferently past the bank entrance but didn't look in. He placed the box key into the silver door lock and swung open the door which shielded Jackie's face from the man in the car. He picked up the receiver and spoke quickly into the receiver.

"This is Officer Monyhan on beat nine. There's a possible robbery in progress at the First National Bank, Washington and Mass Ave. There's a car outside with its engine running, a suspicious-looking fella behind the wheel."

A voice responded immediately, "Roger on that. Backup is on the away."

Jackie hung up, casually closed the box, locked it and put the key back in his shirt pocket. He turned and walked back toward the bank, appearing as if he was going to cross Massachusetts Avenue. When he was a few steps from the bank's entrance he heard a loud noise as two men backed out the door, each firing shots. Jackie ducked around the side of the bank building and withdrew his gun, releasing the safety.

The two robbers didn't see him until he jumped out and shouted, "Police officer, drop your guns and hold your hands high." One of the gunmen turned and fired off two shots at Jackie, who instinctively dropped to one knee and fired back at the robbers. Jackie's bullets found their marks and one man sprawled onto the sidewalk, blood pouring from his chest. This happened so quickly that the second robber didn't have a chance to turn before Jackie fired two more shots, hitting him in the leg and chest. He dropped his gun and started crawling to the getaway car. The driver, seeing that the situation was hopeless, gunned the car into traffic and tried to escape. He didn't get very far before he smashed into a transit upright. His head snapped forward and he hit the steering wheel and lay limp.

At the same time, three patrol cars approached and surrounded the crime scene. Jackie found himself sitting on the sidewalk, leaning against the side of the building, breathing heavily as the adrenaline seeped from his body. Sweat dripped down his face. He let his gun slip from his hand. Tom Breenan, the District Supervisor, jumped from one of the cars and ran toward Jackie. Jackie tried to get up but fell back against the building.

Breenan bent down over Jackie and lightly touched his shoulder. "Are you hit?" he asked.

Jackie looked at him. All he said was, "Yeah," and passed out.

Jackie was taken to Boston City Hospital and treated for shock and a gunshot wound to his left shoulder. Kathleen was called and she arrived at the hospital just as Jackie was being taken to his private room where he would spend the night. She relaxed as she saw his smiling face. He reached out from under the covers and grasped her hand, squeezing it tightly. She returned the squeeze and kissed him gently on the forehead.

Kathleen stayed outside his room as the orderlies and nurses transferred Jackie to the bed. The Captain arrived and told her the story about the robbery and how professionally Jackie had reacted. He also told her that the doctors had said that Jackie would have no permanent physical damage but wanted to keep him overnight for observation. Most likely, he would be released at noon tomorrow. Kathleen felt much better now that she knew that Jackie had not been wounded seriously. Just then the nurse opened the door and motioned to Kathleen that she could come in. Jackie was lying on his back but his head was turned toward the door. Although outwardly he looked at ease, his insides were churning. He had gone through a near fatal encounter and was just realizing that he was lucky to be alive. Things could have easily gone the other way—he could be lying on a slab in the morgue. But he couldn't let Kathleen know this. So he reached up and pulled her down and kissed her on the lips, hoping to show her he was in good spirits.

When Kathleen walked into his room she was feeling the same way. She didn't want Jackie to see how scared she was. She was delighted when his right arm came up to grab her hand and pull her gently down and kiss her lovingly on the lips. She looked at him for a few seconds before she whispered, "Are you really all right?"

"Yeah," he whispered back, holding her hand tightly. "Yeah, everything is in one piece. And I think I can walk and chew gum at the same time," he answered, finding it difficult to talk. He felt so very tired. "But it was one hell of an experience."

Kathleen released her hand. She walked over toward the window to get a chair. She dragged it over next to Jackie and sat down. There was a tap at the door and a nurse came in with a small cup filled with pills, a water pitcher and a glass.

"Hello, Mr. Monyhan. I have some medications for you." She approached the bed and extended her left hand to show them the pills. As she placed the pitcher and glass on the moveable table next to the bed she added, "The purple pill is to ease the pain and the yellow ones are to help you sleep. We can also bring you something to eat right away if you want. The pills will work better if you have food in your stomach."

"Okay," said Jackie, finding it more difficult to concentrate on what she had just said. "About the only thing I could handle right now is a ham and cheese sandwich and a cup of coffee, if that's okay."

The nurse smiled and said, "You're easy to please. I'll see what I can do," and left the room.

Jackie turned to face Kathleen, knowing that they had to discuss what had happened as soon as possible. He reached over and grabbed her hand again. "When I was working on the waterfront, there was always the chance of getting hurt. Don't you remember me telling you that longshoring was the most hazardous job in the country?"

"Yes," replied Kathleen. "But there weren't any people carrying guns."

"I know," said Jackie. "But we knew all of this when I changed jobs. Even if I took the fireman's job, that could be hazardous, too."

"I know," said Kathleen. "But I guess I'm still a little in shock." After a few moments of silence she added with a little smile, "Tomorrow I know I'll feel better, especially when you're home."

Jackie didn't answer. He was already fast asleep. Gently, she pulled the blanket over his shoulders and kissed his cheek. She was sure that he would be asleep for the night. She walked back to the chair, made herself as comfortable as possible, and tried to rest. As she relaxed her body and mind she finally came to terms with what had happened. This was the last thought she had as she drifted in and out of a fitful sleep for the next seven hours.

It was 7 a.m. and they both awoke to a roomful of doctors and nurses. They had Jackie's chart and were talking quietly with each other.

Kathleen pulled herself to a sitting position. "What's going on?"

Dr. Sheffield turned and answered, "Everything seems to be all right, Mrs. Monyhan, so I think Mr. Monyhan can go home at noon. You lost quite a lot of blood, Mr. Monyhan, but you're a healthy young man. You'll be running around the block again before long. You might feel tired for a few days, but that's normal. I'll sign your discharge papers now. I'll also write you a prescription to help with the pain. When they are gone, you can take aspirin, as much as needed." After closing the chart he looked at both of them and added with mock seriousness, "And I would also prescribe a good breakfast. I'll make sure you get one. Actually, I'll order big breakfasts for both of you."

Both Jackie and Kathleen said, "Thank you," as the doctor handed the prescription to Kathleen. Jackie and Kathleen were left to themselves. Kathleen broke the silence.

"Well, Mr. Policeman, I better get myself washed up a little. May I use your facilities?"

"Of course, Mrs. Policeman. But don't hog the bathroom."

When Jackie arrived home to their apartment he felt much weaker than he thought he would. He had to sit down on the sofa as soon as he entered the living room.

"God, I feel so rung out. Me, the strong guy who's never had a day in the hospital before."

"Yeah, you big baby," joked Kathleen. "I suppose you'll want breakfast in bed from now on."

"Hey, that's not a bad idea," he laughed. "You can take a few days off from work, can't you?"

"Of course. Anything you say, big shot. Just explain that to my boss. Well, come on, I suppose I've got to pamper you for a few days anyway. But just don't get used to it."

Slowly, they climbed the stairs together to the second floor. Kathleen opened the door to the bedroom and held it for him. He felt terrible. He walked into the bedroom, turned and tried to gently ease himself onto the bed. Kathleen had to help him to lie down as his shoulder was now very painful. Jackie had been sober for many years and had never gotten into the drug scene. But the pain medications had made him high and killed the pain, almost like being a drunk again. A nurse had administered them every four hours so he had no control over them in the hospital. But here at home he could feel the pain increasing as it got closer to the next dosage.

Jackie's recovery was slower then expected. It was two additional days before he could get out of bed. Kathleen tried to get him to eat but he had no appetite. He drank a lot of fluids which helped some. He had a number of telephone calls from friends as well as from some policemen he didn't even know. He knew that when a cop gets shot, the whole force feels it. On the third day he was able to go downstairs on his own. He drank some coffee and had a slice of toast, loaded with butter. He trudged into the living room and collapsed onto the sofa in front of the TV. The news was just beginning and he propped himself up on a pillow to watch it. The first segment of the news was about JFK and the missiles located in Cuba. The tension was building between the U.S. and U.S.S.R and Kennedy was demanding that the missiles be removed immediately. Up until now there had been no response from the Kremlin. The announcer said that they would report on any changes as they happened. After a few ads, the announcer reported that the Boston Police Department was going to award a Silver Medal to Patrolman Jackie Monyhan for his courageous work in stopping the bank robbery on Washington Street in the South End. The ceremony would take place at Faneuil Hall, after Thanksgiving. Jackie had already been called by the Police Superintendent so he wasn't surprised by the announcement.

Kathleen had been standing behind the sofa as the tribute was announced. She reached around and hugged Jackie. "You're a hero, my hero!" She sat down next to him, then kissed him with all the energy she had. Jackie returned the kiss with equal intensity. They held each other without saying a word. He wanted to make love to her right here but didn't know how Kathleen felt. His question was answered when Kathleen pulled her sweater over her head and released her bra. The phone rang twice but no one answered it. Sometimes making love is the best medicine in the world.

Jackie wanted to return to work the following week but first he had to go through a probationary period because he had fired his weapon. It was mandatory. He was sent to Division Six and rode a patrol car with Larry Flaherty for a few weeks. Most of the time they patrolled Broadway from the Point to Dot Avenue. Usually, the 8 to 4 shift wasn't too busy so Jackie had more time to mend. Although he was still a rookie, he was starting to read some of the police manuals so he would be ready for the sergeant's exam when he became eligible. He and Larry got along well. They had also played football against each other in the Boston Park League. Both of them still looked in shape to still be able to play football. After two weeks of this, Jackie returned to his own station house in the South End. During his first week there he had desk duty which meant he answered phones, filed reports, directed people to the correct office. Finally, his probation was over and he returned to his walking beat.

THE WORLD
OF
A DETECTIVE

CHAPTER 12

▼

Jackie had worked long and hard but it was over. He received his detective's shield on May 14, 1966. He had been on the force since 1957. He had been shot, beat up, almost kidnapped, but he wouldn't trade his job for anything. Becoming a policeman was the second best decision he ever made. Of course, the first was marrying Kathleen. They continued to live in Charlestown, buying a nice house on Warren Street near the famous Warren Tavern restaurant. Kathleen continued to work for New England Tele.

The award ceremony was held at police headquarters on Berkley Street. There were a few dignitaries present and many members of the elite police administration, including evening shift commander, Jimmy O'Neil. He had given Jackie much needed guidance during Jackie's early years. Immediately after the ceremony Jackie and Kathleen went to a small party at the Warren Tavern with a group of close friends. Kathleen and Jackie arrived home about 9:30 p.m. and couldn't wait to get out of their clothes and make love. That was the frosting on the cake. Their love had grown endlessly over the years. They were looking forward to having children and growing old slowly but together. Jackie turned the lights out about 11:00. No Tonight Show this evening.

Jackie's first day of his new job was actually at night. Rookie detectives were always assigned to the 12 midnight to 8 a.m. shift. This would be a difficult change for Jackie but, as always, he would adjust. Kathleen would have to adjust to this new schedule also, because she would be leaving for work when Jackie would be arriving home. They hoped that they would have a few hours in the early evening to enjoy each other's company.

The first day was spent in the area around Field's Corner Station. Jackie arrived at his new posting at 11:30 p.m. He had been informed that rookies get the coffee and doughnuts during the first week of duty. Wanting to start off on the right foot, he stopped at Dunkin' Donuts and bought enough to feed the whole squad.

Lt. Joe Malvesti, the boss of the Detective Division, introduced Jackie to his seven coworkers: Nick Solomonte, Sly Williams, Dickie Biggs, George Santos, Pete Harris, Sylvio Sanchez and Titus Macomber. Their ages ranged between 26 and 60, although the oldest detective, Peter Harris, was in better condition than anyone else in the squad. The lieutenant moved them into the conference room to go over the evening's assignments. He teamed Jackie with Nick Solomonte because Nick was a competent and experienced detective who loved the job and followed the rules. Plus, he owed Joe Malvesti one. Three years ago Joe had saved his life in a shoot-out in a playground near Field's Corner. Jackie would hear this story many times.

Nick Solomonte was 52 years old and had been a detective for over 20 years. He was about 5'10" and weighed in at 185. His slight paunch was offset by his muscular arms and shoulders, the result of his part time job at the Northampton Meat Market where he lifted heavy boxes of pork and beef. As they sat in the conference room Nick took from his pocket a few index cards and a short, stubby pencil. He wrote the date at the top of one of the cards and waited for Lt. Malvesti to begin speaking.

The Lieutenant looked at his clip board and began reading off the assignments for that evening. There were two murders from the previous night. These were assigned to Williams and Biggs. The rest were told to continue on the cases that they were already working on. Nick looked at his tattered index cards and passed one card to Jackie and pointed to the top line on which was scrawled, "180 Commonwealth Ave, Apartment 26—broken into—many gold and silver items taken. Check out pawn shops in the Dorchester and South Boston area."

Nick told Jackie to check out a car for their use and then meet him outside. Jackie walked down to the garage and asked the sergeant on duty about the procedure for taking a car. Sergeant Dean, a 25 year veteran, pointed to a clipboard on the counter and said to fill out the info, sign it and then he would give him one. "Some of these cars are in tough shape, rookie, but I'll get you a good one."

Dean walked into the garage and talked with a man in blue coveralls that were covered with oil stains and grease. The man pointed toward a freshly washed unmarked cruiser. "She's ready to roll. Take her." Dean jumped in, started the car and drove toward Jackie.

Jackie moved over to the passenger seat as Nick came out the back door of the station. Nick climbed in and started the engine. He put the car in gear and said with enthusiasm, "Okay, partner! Let's hope it's an easy night."

As the night wore on, in between visits to various pawn shops which hadn't turned up anything, Jackie's mind drifted. His thoughts kept returning to the night Joey Mons was killed. He had just returned from a wonderful day with Kathleen. They had said good night and he was walking down Chelsea Street when he heard the groaning from behind Doherty's Tavern. There in the weeds he had found Joey's dying body. Jackie had bent down closer to him and Joey had whispered the name of his killer before he died. He remembered his run from both the police and the mobs. Why didn't they ever find Joey's killer?

During the course of the evening, Nick noticed several times that Jackie was staring straight ahead through the car's windshield, but not looking at anything in particular. Finally, Nick couldn't stand it any longer.

"For Christ's sake, Jackie, where is your head tonight? Have a fight with your wife, or something?"

Jackie suddenly woke up and remembered where he was.

"Oh, shit, I'm sorry," replied Jackie and he meant it. "I've got a lot of things on my mind."

"Well, you better lose them when you're out with me," Nick said with a bit of an edge. He waited a few seconds before he added in a friendlier sounding voice, "I need all the help I can get, you know. This driving around looking for something to happen is a real demanding job."

Jackie laughed at Nick's attempt at humor. "You're right. Won't happen again. It's just that I keep thinking about a murder that I was involved in years ago. He was a good friend of mine, guy who taught me the ropes on the waterfront. The anniversary is tomorrow. We never found out who killed him or even why."

Nick waited for a few seconds, then said, "Why don't you tell me more. That is, if you want to."

For the next 15 minutes Jackie told Nick all about Joey Mons, as well as his own brief involvement with the Charlestown and North End mobs.

When Jackie was finished, Nick glanced over at him. "So, now that you're a detective, I suppose you want to find the son of a bitch."

"Yeah," said Jackie. "That would sure make my day."

"Maybe you should just let the dead rest," said Nick. "There isn't much you can do about it now anyway, after all these years."

"But, that's it," replied Jackie. "Now that I'm a detective, maybe I can."

"Well, you'll get over that fast enough. Sometimes a case never gets solved."

Jackie said nothing. He didn't want to antagonize his partner on their first night together. But he had made up his mind long ago that someday he would find Joey's killer.

As they approached one of their final stops, the Lucky Seven Pawnshop at the corner of D and Old Colony Avenue in South Boston, Nick pulled over by the curb, shut off the engine and looked at Jackie. "When we go in, let me do the talking and pay attention to what I say. I want you to learn the right way to do things."

Jackie followed Nick inside. It was a cramped, dusty place, cluttered with all kinds of small items in glass cases. There was a single, ceiling fixture in the center of the room which didn't produce much light. It hadn't been cleaned for years. The bottom of what once had been a clear-glass shade was littered with the remains of dead bugs. A tall, skinny man, dressed all in black, stood behind the glass at the back, looking at a bracelet with a jeweler's loop. He looked up briefly and then back down. He appeared to be annoyed that he was being interrupted. His gaunt, angular features made him look like someone who had enjoyed too many drugs over the years. He was surprisingly clean shaven. His stringy, black hair was spotted with grey strands. He looked to be about 60, but was probably more like 40.

Nick showed him his badge and introduced himself and Jackie. Jackie fumbled through his pockets, searching for his badge. When he did find it, he pulled it out so fast that it became detached from its leather case, ending up on the floor. Quickly, he picked it up and showed it to the skinny man. Nick was having a difficult time hiding his smile, recalling his first day on the job, doing almost the identical thing.

"You run this place?" asked Nick.

"Yeah, that's me. Here all the time."

"What's your name?"

"Frank DeMilo."

"Okay, Frank. Maybe you can help us out." The annoyed expression on Frank's face didn't change. Nick took three photos of jewelry from his pocket and pushed them through the opening. "Have you seen any of these?"

Frank took off the jeweler's loop and moved his eyes down to the counter and said, "No!" Nick told him to look again. Frank didn't try any harder but only repeated his answer, "No!"

"Okay, Frank," said Nick. "I want an inventory of everything you've got, and I mean everything, that you've taken in during the past two weeks."

The two stared at each other. Now he had Frank's attention. This time he bent down closer to the pictures and squinted at them for several seconds. He straightened up while pointing to the photo of the necklace that had a diamond pennant attached to it.

"Yeah, I saw this one the other day, Tuesday. A woman, a real good looking redhead, was in here Tuesday trying to pawn that necklace. She had an ass on a pair of legs that was out of sight. I smelled something fishy so I didn't make her an offer. It seems that my gut feeling was right."

Nick asked, "She say anything else?"

"She started to bargain about price, but I still said, no. Finally, she asked, 'Do you know any place I can get rid of this?' Of course, I said I didn't. She got angry, grabbed the necklace and stormed out the door."

"Was she alone?" asked Nick.

"I think there must have been a car waiting for her outside," Frank said.

"How do you know that?"

"Right after she left, I heard a car door close and a car pull away fast."

Nick took a card from his inside pocket and handed it to Frank. "If you see these items or the redhead again, give me a call. We'll leave the photos here in case you get lucky." As he walked toward the door, Nick turned and added, "My partner here, Jackie, will be back to check on you next week."

"Yeah, sure, anytime," Frank answered, still annoyed, as he watched the detectives exit the shop.

As they got into the car, Nick said to Jackie, "I think we stumbled on something. We'll have to keep our eyes on this place. And you did nice work. Most rookies would have opened their mouths, just to let me know they were there."

"Thanks, Nick," said Jackie. "And I can hardly wait to stop by here again next week."

Nick only answered with a smile.

When the shift was over, Jackie said goodbye to Nick and drove to Charlestown. The time was 8:00 a.m. and Kathleen would have already left for work. Jackie saw a note on the kitchen table. He picked it up and read it. "Missed you—Love You—see you tonight." Jackie climbed the stairs, entered their bedroom, stripped off his clothes and fell into bed. Sleep came quickly but the dreams came just as fast. Joey Mons was serving him a drink in the Eight Bells. Then he was lying dead in the grass behind Doherty's Tavern. All of a sudden there was a black car speeding up the street with a man hanging out the rear window shooting at him. Jackie awoke, soaked in sweat. A few minutes passed and he fell asleep again. This time, there were no dreams or nightmares.

He awoke about 3 p.m. and fixed himself some scrambled eggs, toast and coffee. He cleaned the kitchen, found the morning paper and went into the living room to read it. Kathleen would be home about 6. There would be plenty of time to make love and have a light supper, too.

CHAPTER 13

▼

During the past twenty years, the Hayes-McCormick Gang had expanded and become more organized. They were still heavy into bookmaking, truck hijacking, stealing, fencing, and loan sharking. They had also gained control of the drug trade in Charlestown and parts of Everett. Tommy Hayes was in charge of the non-drug business while Mike McCormick took care of the drug trade. Each had a number of associates, a sort of chain of command. Tommy's four under-bosses were Bernie O'Brien, Peter Sobel, Jerry Sabalock and Mik O'Koren. They made sure that everyone under them obeyed the rules and didn't skim any money. Everyone made good money, however, but there was always someone who wanted more. They established a set of rules and specific punishments when any of those rules was violated.

Mike McCormick used a similar procedure but he had many more people under his control. The game plan was to keep the drugs and money as far away as possible from the upper echelon. Sam Peters, Joey Angelo, Tim Shea and Jim Sullivan were his bosses. They made the major drug buys from four different sources. Then they sold them to the next tier of workers who, in turn, sold them to the street workers who went into the projects to sell to the users. The market price varied from shipment to shipment, but there was always a huge profit.

Hayes and McCormick continued to work independently from the North End Mob but still paid a gratuity to Carmine. Both groups seemed to be satisfied with this arrangement.

The police authorities knew quite a bit of what was happening, receiving most of their tips from a few gang members who were trying to please both sides at the same time. The trouble was, no one was willing to swear to it in court. The closest the police came to making a breakthrough was when they arrested Charlie Wilson for possession.

Charlie Wilson had a colorful past and one which was well known to those who lived in Charlestown. He had been a great athlete at Malden Catholic, making all-scholastic in football and baseball. He even had a tryout with the St. Louis Cardinals but his fielding was weak. But at least he had a tryout. He was always bigger than the other kids, finally rounding out at 6'2" and 210 lbs with a great head of blond hair and a smile that the girls fell for. He played a mean game of softball. Some of his home runs were famous, especially the one that almost hit St. Catherine's Church. After he graduated from high school he went to work for Boston Edison. After two years of this, Charlie left, or was fired, from his job. Eventually, he became part of the Hayes-McCormick Gang. Charlie became their chief enforcer. He gave up drinking and drugging but still continued to gamble, getting in debt, deeper and deeper. Charlie was into them for about $2000 in gambling debt. To help pay it off they used him to collect money from borrowers who didn't pay on time. Charlie's first approach was simple. He asked them, do you have the money? Any answer but yes brought a swift punch to the victim's kidney section, then a sharp kick in the groin area. With most customers this worked. Charlie inflicted enough pain to make the victim pay by his next visit. Nobody wanted to put the borrower in the hospital because then the poor slob wouldn't be able to pay off his debt.

During this time, the Gang let Charlie place bets of any amount, at any time. This was to suck Charlie in so deep that he couldn't get out. They even let him win a few hands of poker or blackjack so he wouldn't realize what was going on.

Most people believed that Charlie wasn't involved in any murders but this changed when Freddie Stone's body washed up on the Chelsea side of the oily river. Freddie had been beaten to death with a baseball bat. This was another one of Charlie's methods to persuade reluctant clients to pay. This time he had carried it too far. The rumor was that Freddie and Charlie had had an argument over Maureen, the good looking one of the Foley sisters. She was a bleached blond and had a body like Marilyn Monroe, only more so. She most certainly fought any dress that she could squeeze into. After this incident most people stayed away from Charlie.

The police planned to offer Charlie a deal, in exchange for information. George Dolan, a lawyer for Tommy Hayes, arranged bail for Charlie. He was released within three hours of his arrest. Charlie walked out of the station at 3:00 p.m., took a cab to Chelsea and was last seen at the Italian Athletic Club with Pooch Pucina, a low-life gang member who was a drinking buddy of Charlie's.

They weren't seen again until their frozen bodies bounced onto the deck of the Black Heron in Antwerp, several weeks later. The police aggressively pursued the case but couldn't make any headway. This only tightened the grip that the Hayes-McCormick Gang had on its workers.

Jackie left his Charlestown home at 10:30 p.m. to drive to the Fields Corner station. On his second night he and Nick reviewed the list of stolen items. Lt. Malvesti came into the room and signaled for Nick to come to his desk. "Are you still working on the pawn shop case?" he asked.

"Yes," replied Nick.

Malvesti handed him a sheet of paper. It was a report from another precinct, listing jewelry that was found on a robbery suspect. "Check these items with your master list. See if there are any similarities. I think there might be."

Nick walked back to his desk which was facing Jackie's. "Here," he said, handing Jackie a copy of the new list of stolen items. "See if any of these match the ones on our list. Jackie eagerly pulled out his copy of the stolen items and went to work.

It didn't take long to see that most of the items on the lists matched. He looked at the suspect's name: Phil Merchinson from Somerville.

"I've got a few matches, too," said to Nick. "Let's see where this guy is being held."

Nick called the Berkeley Street Station where the arrest took place and asked for detective Frank Sullivan. Within a few minutes Sullivan was on the line, razzing Joe about the Knicks, telling him that they should lower the basket so that the Knicks might have a chance to win a game. Nick, for some unknown reason, was a N.Y. Knicks fan. Nick said, "That wouldn't help the Celtics anyway because they couldn't find the basket no matter where it was."

They both laughed. Nick said, "I need a favor, Sully."

"What now?" answered Frank. "Anything to help an old buddy." Nick and Frank had been rookies in the police academy together.

"You arrested a guy named Phil Merchinson for theft," Nick said.

"That's right," answered Frank. "He got stopped for speeding and running a red. When he and his lady friend started bad-mouthing the cop that stopped him, he pulled them in. There was a bagful of jewelry hidden in his car. We think that some of the stuff came from a place in our precinct."

"So there was somebody with him?"

"Yeah, a flashy redhead, but she didn't have a record."

"Flashy redhead?" said Nick. "That sounds like the woman at that last pawn shop we stopped at last night. She tried to get rid of one of the stolen necklaces."

"Which pawn shop was that?"

"The Lucky Seven, corner of D and Old Colony."

"Great. We'll check that out."

"Where are Merchinson and the redhead being held?" Nick asked.

"Nowhere," answered Frank. "They're both out on the street. They were bailed out by a lawyer right after the arraignment. I think he lives in Somerville or Charlestown."

Nick said, "Who's the lawyer?"

"Papers say it's George Dolan," replied Frank.

"Dolan," said Nick. "That's a pretty high priced lawyer for a two-bit jewel thief."

"That's what I thought," answered Frank. "He's also Tommy Hayes' personal lawyer."

"Really," Nick said with surprise. "That's interesting. I've got an address for this Merchinson guy. I'll have one of the day guys check it out tomorrow." Nick said thanks to Frank and hung up. Nick relayed the information to Jackie.

"Merchinson," said Jackie. "I went to school with a Merchinson. There were brothers. I lost track after high school. I think my brother, Paul, was close to one of them."

"It's kind of an odd name. Why don't you look into it."

"Will do," answered Jackie.

At 3:17 a.m. a call came in regarding an assault that had taken place in a local tavern. Malvesti told Nick and Jackie to check it out. Jackie wrote down the address of the bar. Nick drove the car down Dorchester Ave. at about 30 miles per hour. He wasn't in much of a rush. The fight would be over anyway and everyone would say that they were in the men's' room when it happened. He hoped that no one was injured. That would mean a trip to City Hospital and it was getting near the end of their shift. As they pulled into the curb in front of the Royal Shamrock Café they saw an ambulance parked outside. The rear door was open which meant that they hadn't taken anyone out yet. If the person was conscious they would be able to get a statement before he was taken to the hospital.

The detectives walked into the bar and saw a small crowd looking at someone on the floor. The ambulance techs were applying bandages to the head of a man who looked to be in his early fifties. He tried to focus his eyes on the detectives, but was too drunk. The cut on his head had stopped bleeding but it probably needed a few stitches to close it. Nick asked a man who had on an apron what happened. He shrugged his shoulders and said that Timothy was drunk and fell getting off the stool, trying to get to the head.

"Are you sure that's how it happened?" asked Nick. "We got a report of a fight."

The bartender said, "No, that's a lot of bull. Who said that?"

"A cop," answered Nick.

"Well, he was wrong," said the bartender as he picked up a broom and started to sweep the floor.

Nick looked at the bartender and said with a sarcastic smile, "Don't call us when you really need us. Next time, we may not come or be too busy." The bartender continued to attack the floor with his broom.

Jackie cleared his throat and asked "Why are you still open? It's after closing time."

The bartender glared at Jackie, "Can't you see we're cleaning up? There aren't any drinks on the bar, are there?"

Jackie knew that there weren't any but he thought he would remind him. He turned and followed the stretcher outside. The techs were lifting Timothy and the stretcher into the ambulance when Jackie had an idea.

"Hey, guys, wait a minute," Jackie called out to the techs, as he stooped down to the sidewalk and appeared to pick up something. "The guy dropped his wallet."

Jackie walked over to the back of the ambulance and got in, motioning silently to the techs to go outside. When they were outside Jackie approached Timothy. He bent over and straightened out the man's rumpled coat collar and put his hand inside the man's coat.

"Hey, Tim, you fell off a stool, that right?" he asked casually and so only Tim could hear.

"Yeah."

"Really."

"Ya, I do that sometimes," he said slowly, slurring his words.

"Okay, Tim. It's just you and me alone in here, okay? No one else around. Why don't you tell me who did this to you."

Tim was silent.

"Well, what did he look like? Tall? Short? White? Black? Come on Tim. The only way we're going to get this guy is if you tell us. We can get him off the streets so you can come in here again for another drink. You do like to drink, don't you, Tim? Isn't this your favorite drinking place?

Tim looked at Jackie but still said nothing.

"You ever see this guy before?"

"Yeah."

"A regular?"

"No, he just collects … stuff from us."

"Okay."

"If … I tell you … will he … find out?"

"He won't hear it from me."

"You don't … have to tell him … it was me?"

"Course not."

"I only … know his nickname."

"That's okay."

"Around here … guys know him as … PM."

"PM?" Jackie repeated, almost not believing what thoughts jumped into his head.

"Yeah, that's it."

"Okay, Tim. You'll be all right."

As Jackie climbed out of the ambulance he said loudly back to Tim, "Okay, Tim, you got your wallet back. Hope you feel better."

"What was that all about?" asked Nick as they got back into the car and headed back to the station.

"Timothy just told me who did it. Guy known as PM. Would you believe that? PM. I don't know. When he said it, it reminded me what Joey Mons had said to me before he died. I thought it was more like 'pam,' but maybe he was try-ing to say PM, some guy's initials."

"But that was how many years ago? Where's he been all this time?"

"I don't know, but I'm not going to let it go till I find out."

They soon reached the station and Nick parked the car. Running up the steps to the station, Jackie told Nick that he would make out the report, then headed toward his desk. He noticed a small white piece of paper, placed under his phone. He pulled it out and read it. It said, "Call mother-<u>emergency</u>."

Jackie picked up the phone and called his mother's number, trying not to think the worst. She answered on the first ring.

"Hello, mom, what's going on?" he asked anxiously with a sickening feeling growing in the pit of his stomach.

In a choked voice she answered. "Oh, Jackie, your father's in the hospital. He had a heart attack." Then after a few seconds she added, "I need to get to the hospital."

Jackie was stunned. His father always appeared to be in good health. He had stopped drinking a few years ago and had lost weight. He had never complained at all about his health.

"I'll be there as fast as I can, ma. Don't worry," he answered and hung up.

As he drove through town, headed for Charlestown, his mind was racing. His dad had changed so much after he got himself sober. It was almost impossible to remember what a difficult man he had been. The fights with his mother, the times Jackie and his brothers had to go to the barroom to rescue him from a beating or an arrest. How quickly a person can change his life around. And how wonderful when it does.

As he rounded the corner he could see his mother standing at the bottom of the stairs with her sweater in her hand, waving frantically at him as he drove up. The sweater, Jackie thought. His mother wouldn't go anywhere without it, regardless of the weather. His father had given it to her on her first birthday after he got sober. *Oh, God, don't let it end now.*

Quickly his mother got in the car. Jackie leaned over and kissed her on the cheek. "Everything will be all right, ma, just calm down."

He drove fast, but carefully, as he wound his way toward Boston City Hospital on Massachusetts Avenue in the South End. It took no more than 15 minutes before they were parked in a space reserved for emergency room families. Jackie walked fast next to his mother, not knowing what to expect. He could tell by the look on his mother's face that the situation wasn't good. He hoped and prayed for the best, but he had a feeling, a gut feeling, that it wasn't going to be good. They stepped up to the emergency room counter and Jackie asked if they had any information on Matthew Monyhan. The nurse, a young thing that seemed bored with her job, asked, "Are you a relative?"

He glared back at her and replied sharply, "Yes, I'm his son and this is his wife."

The nurse glanced toward the closed door to the emergency room. "Just a minute," she said. "I'll have to get Dr. Winslow. He's the doctor in charge tonight." She walked to the back of the small room and picked up the phone. Her voice came over the speakers: "Dr. Winslow to the front desk."

In less than a minute, a doctor in a white jacket came through the ER doors. He was tall, about 6'3", stocky for a doctor with a red, stringy beard. The nurse at the counter pointed toward Jackie and his mother. The doctor turned and headed in their direction. He introduced himself and motioned for them to sit down at one end of the large waiting room. He lowered his large frame into a chair where he could see both of them. He raised his head and said softly but sincerely, "I am very sorry. It was a massive heart attack. We tried everything, but we couldn't revive Mr. Monyhan. His heart couldn't handle it. He never regained consciousness. I'm so sorry." He paused. "Would you like for me to call Father Callahan? He is a Jesuit priest who lives close by at the St. James Rectory."

Jackie looked at his mother who was in shock. He answered for her, "Yes, that would be good." He reached out and took his mother's hands and pulled her into his large arms. As soon as her head met his shoulder, she started to sob which turned quickly to a torrent of tears. She kept calling her husband's name, as if she thought he would appear.

Dr. Winslow pulled himself to his feet, nodded at Jackie and said in a whisper, "I'll call Father Callahan. He's very good at times like these."

As the sun began to rise, other members of the family arrived at the hospital. Jackie had called Paul, his closest brother, who had called other members and friends of the family. He was the first to arrive at the hospital, followed shortly by Sean and Colleen. Francis Xavier, the youngest child, was the last to arrive. Father Callahan had taken Mrs. Monyhan to the Chapel to say a rosary. Jackie hugged each sibling as they arrived and explained to them what had happened. Each had their own way of dealing with grief.

By noon the body had been released to the McNamara Funeral Home in Charlestown. Jackie and his sister Colleen went there later that day to make the funeral arrangements. Jackie's mother had been given a sedative by Dr. Winslow and was now sleeping. The family was gathered for a short time at the family home and went through the motions of getting the house ready for the day of the funeral where everyone would be invited back to the house. Jackie didn't look forward to this. Some people always ended up getting drunk with arguments and fights usually following.

The wake was set for Wednesday night, 7 to 9 p.m. and Thursday 2 to 4 and 7 to 9 p.m. The funeral mass would be Friday at 9:00 a.m. with the burial at Holy Cross Cemetery in Malden immediately afterwards. When they left McNamara's, Jackie asked Colleen to come to his house for coffee but she declined saying she wanted to stop at their mother's house before she made the trip back to Stoneham. They hugged and said good night. Jackie headed directly home.

Kathleen met him at the door and crushed him with a powerful hug and kiss. "Oh, Jackie, I'm so sorry. I loved your father and I will really miss him." The pent-up tears rolled down Jackie's cheeks as he hugged his wife even closer.

Although it was only 6:30, a line was forming outside McNamara's Funeral Home on Bunker Hill Street. Wakes and funerals in Charlestown were as much a social event as a religious one. It was a day when bad blood was suspended between the good guys and bad guys, the cops and the robbers, the divorced wives and husbands and all other rivalries. Immediately at 7:00 p.m. the front door opened and people walked in to pay their respects. This was the custom, this was the rule, this was the way it was done in Charlestown. Usually the family members and the closest friends were the first to view the body. Visitors would kneel before the casket and say a short prayer, then stop to say a few words to the immediate family. They would then find places in the waiting room or if they were a smoker, go to the smoking room. The conversations would range from serious to witty, depending on the group. At some time during the wake a priest would arrive and say the rosary, slowly, taking his time. Afterwards, visitors would leave so that the family would have some time to themselves.

Things went quite smoothly during the two days of the wake with no troubles, everyone behaving themselves. There were so many people that most of the time it was difficult to find time to just get some fresh air. It was impossible to find a place to sit down. Brothers and sisters, nieces and nephews, aunts and uncles, Charlestown neighbors, co-workers from the police force, former co-workers from the waterfront all formed their own small groups, often acting like they were at a reunion, telling jokes and remembering better days. Sam Sullivan and Myles McDonough were there, two of his father's close longshoremen buddies from many years ago. It was good to see them. They asked him how he liked being on the police force. Was it easy to get used to? Did he have any regrets? Jackie told them that the transition was fairly easy and no, he didn't have any regrets, although he would be glad when he could go on days. Also, he planned to keep paying his union dues in case he did return to the waterfront. Next came a few friends of his mother. They were crying along with her. They said that they were thankful that she had had all those years when Matt was sober. She agreed, with a forced smile.

"God, this is so difficult," Jackie said in a whisper to no one in particular. A voice interrupted his thoughts.

"Hi, Jackie, remember me?"

Jackie turned and looked into the face of a young man who looked very famil-iar, but he couldn't put a name to. The man extended his hand.

"Sal, Salvatore Mons. Joey's brother. We met years ago at the Eight Bells. Just before Joey died.

Jackie smiled and shook his hand. Memories came flooding back.

"Of course, Sal. Where've you been all these years? You seemed to disappear afterwards."

"Yeah, well I got a job working for some guys. Then got transferred out to Chicago."

Sal had definitely changed since that time years ago when Joey had introduced him to Jackie in the Eight Bells. Now he wore glasses and the angular features which Jackie had noticed when they first met had been rounded out by a few pounds. His hair was longer too. He held a black, scally cap in his hand. His short, black leather coat still showed off his muscular physique. He still wore the Marine ring on his left hand.

"What are you doing back here? You miss Charlestown?" Jackie asked with a smile.

"You could say that. No, I got some important business out here for a little while. Then I'll go back to Chicago again. It's a nice town, I like it there." After a few moments Sal added, "Sorry to hear about your father. I didn't know about it till one of the guys told me."

"Thanks. It was sudden, but what can you do?" After an awkward silence Jackie added, "Yeah, maybe someday we'll get to Chicago. Come on over, I want you to meet my wife."

Jackie led Sal through the crowd to where Kathleen was seated and spent the next several minutes talking with them. It wasn't very long before Jackie had to say goodbye to Sal as more visitors came in to pay their respects. Jackie quickly extended his hand to Sal and they shook hands.

"It was good to see you, Sal. Try and stay a little longer next time."

"Yeah, sounds good, Jackie. We'll see how things work out."

Jackie left Sal talking with Kathleen.

Conversations with the family were usually kept short, with awkward smiles and strong handshakes. One conversation, however, which occurred on the sec-ond night, proved to be so unpredictable and astonishing that Jackie repeated it continuously in his mind, analyzing and reviewing it again and again during the following days. It was with a woman who was a friend of Kathleen's. As Jackie approached the two of them in the hall of the funeral home, Kathleen turned to Jackie and introduced her.

"Jackie, this is Lisa Belcher. She and her sister, Janice, both work at the phone company with me." Turning to Lisa, Kathleen continued, "It was so good of you to come tonight, Lisa. Jackie and I appreciate it very much."

"Oh, Kathleen, I know it's hard when your parents pass away. I just wanted to come by and say how sorry I was. I saw the announcement in the paper and had to come. I haven't seen you for a while."

"I know. We've missed you at lunch the last week. How is your new apartment working out?"

"Well, so far it's been fine. At least I haven't been bothered by that creep of a boyfriend who couldn't get it in his head that I didn't want to see him anymore. A real weirdo, Kathleen. I just hope he doesn't bother me anymore. I was even getting scared he would do something, like hit me or something."

"Why haven't you called the police?" asked Kathleen.

"Oh, no," said Lisa. "I don't know what he'd do if he ever found out I did that. I really don't want to get the police involved."

"If you do have problems, just let Jackie know. You know you have a friend in the police department that you can turn to."

Jackie confirmed what his wife had just said, "Of course, Lisa, just let me know if you have trouble and I can make sure he doesn't bother you again."

"Oh, thanks so much, Jackie. And since breaking up with him I've heard so many bad stories about him." Once Lisa got started, she didn't want to stop. "Why do I keep picking up these losers? When he got drunk he really could get nasty. And he could tell such wild stories, I didn't know what was real or what he was making up. At least I hope he was making them up. Beatings and knifings and getting into fights. And I just find out he was in the can for 12 years. He wouldn't tell me for what. When we first started going out he was a lot of fun, loved to play cards. He could stay up all night and just play cards. That's how he got his nickname, PM, 'cuz he stayed up so late. Funny, how they're also his initials."

It was quiet for a few seconds as Jackie ran over in his mind what Lisa had just said. A bell seemed to go off in Jackie's head. Joey Mons' last words came rushing back.

"Lisa, what was your boyfriend's name?"

"Phil, Phil Merchinson."

After the burial on Friday, people were invited back to the Monyhan home for refreshments. Many came but didn't stay long. Jackie had limited the amount of beer and booze on hand so the crowd dispersed rather quickly. Finally the Mony-hans were alone with their sorrow.

The following Monday Jackie returned to work. He brought Nick up to date on Lisa and her boyfriend, PM, otherwise known as Phil Merchinson.

"Let's get more information on this Phil guy. Call around to some other stations. See if we've missed something," Nick said.

Jackie called Tommy Fitzgibbons at Station 15 in Charlestown. "Hi," he said. "This is Jackie Monyhan from the Field's Corner Station."

"Yeah, hi," said Tommy. "What can I do for you?"

"Do you know anything about a Phil Merchinson? He's one of Tommy Hayes' guys. We think he could be involved in an old murder case we're checking out again."

After a few seconds Tommy answered, "Yeah, I know him. He's one of Hayes' guys for sure, but we haven't heard anything about him for the six months. We think he had something to do with Charlie Wilson's and that other guy's disappearance but we couldn't prove it."

"Yeah, I'm not surprised," answered Jackie. Do you have anything else?"

"We have a file," answered Tommy. "I'll make a copy and send it over to you. I'll do it today."

"Thanks, we'd appreciate that," said Jackie and hung up.

"This Phil Merchinson is one classic act. He keeps reappearing like a bad penny. I wonder what he'll do next," said Nick.

"He's dirty, Nick. Some day he's going to run up against somebody who will be tougher than he is. I just hope I'm around to see how it plays out."

When Jackie got to work on Tuesday the information that Tommy Fitzgibbons promised was there. Phil Merchinson's juvenile record was sealed, but there had been a number of arrests for assault and battery over the years. He was found not guilty on most of the charges, except for the most recent one when the guy he was fighting with died. Phil was in Walpole Prison for 12 years. It would have been longer, but his lawyer found that the guy had had a heart condition and he might have died from that. Phil just got out of prison six months ago. He was on probation. He hadn't been keeping his probation appointments, however. The most important item in the folder was Merchinson's picture. Now Jackie had a face to look at. Phil was 45 years old, 5'11" tall, 185 lbs. In the photograph he had short, dark blond hair, blue eyes and a small scar on his left cheek. He didn't graduate from Somerville High School but earned a G.E.D. while in prison. The file stated that he was self employed but it didn't say at what. Jackie closed the file and began to think how he could get close to this guy and find out if he had any-thing to do with Joey Mons' murder. Nick interrupted his thoughts, yelling at him that there had been a robbery at Bradlees' on Morrissey Boulevard and they had to go and interview some witnesses. Jackie went to get a car, then drove around to pick up Nick at the front of the station.

CHAPTER 14

▼

Jackie and Nick continued on nights for the next two weeks, then rotated to the day shift, 8 a.m. to 4 p.m. This was important to Jackie. Kathleen was four months pregnant and would need more of his support during the coming months.

Work became increasingly busy. Jackie had talked with a few people, including one of his brothers, about the Merchinsons and found out some additional information. It seemed that Phil was the black sheep of the family. He had been suspended from Somerville High School because he hit another student over the head with a lunch tray and struck a teacher who tried to break up the fight. He never returned to school. Six months later he was arrested for stealing a car and attempting to run down a police officer who was trying to stop him. He was sentenced to two years in Norfolk, but only did 18 months before he was released for good behavior. While in prison he took high school courses and passed his equivalency exam. It looked as if he had turned a corner and changed his behavior, but a year or so later, according to a detective friend from the 15th precinct, he was seen hanging around Tommy Hayes at a Bruins game. Boston Garden was where Tommy held many of his meetings. It wasn't exactly private but it did have lots of noise. On the other hand, no one ever saw anybody at the Boston Garden, especially Tommy and his crew.

Jackie had the day off but he was still thinking about the case. He was pondering all this when Katherine came out from the kitchen, "Let's go out for a pizza tonight. I don't feel like cooking."

"Okay," answered Jackie. "We'll go to the Regina."

"That's a great idea."

It had been a rainy spring and tonight was no exception. They left the house about 6:30 p.m. Jackie held the door open for Kathleen as she hurried down the steps and struggled somewhat to get in the car.

"I'll be glad when we finally get rid of all this rain," Kathleen said, sounding depressed.

As Jackie drove he looked over at Katherine and said softly with a smile, "You look beautiful. Being pregnant only makes you look better, you know."

"Okay, wise guy, stop thinking beyond the pizza. You know my condition is delicate."

Jackie grinned and mockingly said, "How could you think such evil things about me?"

Kathleen made a stern face, "It's because I know you so well."

Jackie turned left at the end of the bridge and drove down Endicott Street. "I think I'll park at Angelo's place tonight. He owes me a few favors for the parking tickets I took care of."

"On the take again, Monyhan," said Kathleen, shaking her head and looking away as she smiled.

"No," he answered. "Well, not exactly."

Jackie waved to Angelo Satani as he pulled into the small parking lot next to station's office.

"Are you slumming tonight or are just interested in getting a good meal?" Angelo hollered as he collected money from a customer and headed toward Jackie's car. "Hi, good looking," he said to Kathleen as she climbed out of the front seat. "It's a shame you had to marry this Mick when a handsome Italian guy like me was available."

"Yeah," answered Kathleen as she gave Angelo a playful hug. "But you know my spaghetti sauce is lousy so it wouldn't have been such a good deal."

As Jackie walked to Kathleen's side of the car he tossed the keys to Angelo saying "Don't you dare take the Malibu for a joy ride."

"Are you kidding?" answered Angelo. "I wouldn't want to embarrass myself in front of my friends, riding in this old jalopy."

"Ha," laughed Jackie. "By the way, we're going to the Regina. We'll be gone a few hours. Will you still be open when we get back?"

"Sure will, partner," Angelo yelled back as he headed over to another car pulling up to the pumps. As Jackie and Kathleen walked up Hanover Street they didn't notice the green sedan parked on the other side of the street.

After dinner Jackie and Kathleen didn't want to head right back to the car. It was rather cool but the rain had stopped. They spent some time walking up and down the quaint streets in the North End, looking in the shops and just enjoying holding hands and being together. They stopped briefly along Salem Street and acted like tourists, reading the signs at the Old North Church, made famous by Longfellow's poem about the first major battle of the Revolutionary War. This Italian enclave of the North End was home to many immigrants and their descendants, where you could still hear Italian spoken on the streets every day.

"What a beautiful evening," said Kathleen, when they had reached the car an hour later.

Angelo had left but his younger brother, Dom, was there and he handed Jackie the keys. "Angelo said he would put the charge on your tab." Quickly he added, "Only kidding, only kidding."

Jackie smiled, "I know what you mean. See you later." He opened the door for Kathleen, then ran to the driver's side, shivering, "Boy, did it get cold," as he hurriedly got behind the wheel.

"What a wimp," said Kathleen, who enjoyed the cooler air. "I remember when you worked outside all the time and the cold didn't bother you at all."

"Yeah, I know, but sometimes the money was better," said Jackie as he started the Malibu. Kathleen cuddled up to Jackie, saying, "It was the right choice, Jackie. Don't ever forget that."

Jackie grinned while looking at her and said, "Don't I know it. Two great choices I've made in my short life. The first one was picking you and the second was leaving the waterfront." Jackie was about to drive away when he noticed a note tucked under the windshield wiper. "What, did Angelo leave me a love note?" asked Jackie. He got out of the car and pulled out the piece of paper, which had been folded a few times. It had only a few words handwritten on it. "DO YOU REMEMBER JOEY MONS, COP?" Jackie quickly looked around the neighborhood but did not see anyone or anything that looked suspicious. Jackie and Kathleen looked seriously at each other.

"What a way to end a perfect evening," Kathleen said. Neither one saw the green sedan pull away from the curb.

Jackie and Kathleen worked very hard to keep Jackie's mother comfortable in her own home where she continued to live by herself. Jackie's sisters and their families, along with his brothers, invited her to many family gatherings. The women always prepared a nice dinner, usually on Sundays, then finished cleaning up the dishes as the men talked about the latest news in sports. Mr. Monyhan's memory was always present but as the days and weeks wore on, talking about him became easier. Much of the conversation, to everyone's relief, centered around the impending birth. Katherine's stomach was now getting noticeably larger with each passing day. She had quit her job on May 1st.

The police were able to positively identify Phil Merchinson as the jewelry thief they were looking for. The address on his record proved to be non existent, however. He had disappeared after his bail was reduced and his lawyer, who was indeed Tommy Hayes' lawyer, had posted it. The Charlestown and Somerville cops were keeping an eye out for him but with no results. He was keeping a very low profile which caused some concern to Jackie. His redheaded girl friend hadn't been seen either.

Jackie was thinking a lot about Phil Merchinson, wanting especially to question him about the night Joey was murdered. Nick kept telling him that he had to have patience, that there would no doubt be a break in the case.

The break came during a Red Sox baseball game on a Sunday afternoon in June. Jackie had invited some friends and family, including his mother, over to watch.

During a short commercial break Jackie went into the kitchen. He was mixing up some drinks when Packie O'Brien joined him. Packie was the local tattletale, a guy who seemed to know everybody and their business. He lived in Charlestown but had worked in Polcari's coffee shop in the North End since he was a kid. He was like an uncle to Jackie, having been a good friend to Jackie's father. He usually had some local gossip to spread. Packie didn't drink too much and whatever he said could surprisingly have some truth attached to it.

"Hey, Jackie," he said as he pulled up a stool and sat down. "I heard a story today that you might find interesting. Joey-the-Shoes Connolly was in Doherty's last Friday night and he was fall-down drunk, I mean, really getting kind of obnoxious, bragging about a guy he knew named Phil. Met him at the Eight Bell's some night last week. Kind of bragging, you know, saying 'Phil this and Phil that." He said this Phil guy was drinking quite a bit, that he was smooth, that he could disappear in a crowd and his own mother couldn't identify him. Bragging that he was part of Tommy Hayes' Gang but did his work very secret-like. Said he was doing things even Tommy didn't know anything about, like 'making certain people disappear if they rubbed him the wrong way.' Anyway, Connolly said you'd be surprised at the number of people he had killed. One in particular would be of interest to the cops in Charlestown. Seems years ago the guy got into an argument with a certain bartender. Phil said some things to the guy, like threats, that something could happen to him, like a lot of others. I guess the bartender was trying to get Phil to leave and Phil didn't really want to. Phil backed off when the bartender's brother came in and sat down at the bar."

Jackie put his glass down and stared at Packie. "When did you say this argument took place?"

"Oh, a lot of years ago. Guess this Phil didn't care who heard it after all this time." Packie swallowed his drink of Old Thompson, went to the bathroom, then came back into the kitchen. Jackie was lost in thought as he finished mixing the rest of the drinks.

"Was there anyone else there near Connolly when he was talking about this Phil guy?" Jackie asked.

"Hell, I don't know. But you know the Eight Bell's is always crowded on a Friday night. Someone always starts up a poker game in the back room. Phil's a pretty good player, according to Connolly anyway. Phil wanted to get another game going and Mons, the bartender, wanted to close up." Packie was silent for several seconds. Jackie continued to stare at him without saying a word. Packie broke the silence.

"Hey, but you know how Connolly is when he's drinking like that," Packie added with a nervous laugh as he got up from his stool. "Loud, no one wants to be with him because he's so crazy, unpredictable. One minute he's calling you the greatest guy in the world. Then all of a sudden he puts a gun to your head or hits you with a beer bottle."

"Yeah," answered Jackie. "You remember what happened to Buddy O'Keefe. He's in a wheelchair now. He was just kidding around and called Connolly an asshole. But tell me again exactly what he said."

Packie repeated his story, almost word for word. Jackie nodded his head and said thanks. He picked up the drinks and headed to the living room. "We should get back. I want to see how the game is going."

Jackie had no idea how the rest of game went because his mind was in another world. He was trying to piece it all together. Joey Mons trying to identify his killer as he lay dying in the weeds, Lisa Belcher at the wake connecting PM with Phil Merchinson, the jewelry robbery, Timothy's identification, now Packie O'Brien's story about Joey-the-Shoes at the Eight Bells. Jackie also remembered the days just after Joey was killed when Carmine in the North End Mob had told Sgt. O'Neil that if he wanted to find Joey's killer, he better look for someone in Tommy Hayes' Gang. All the loose ends were now getting put together.

Before he knew it the game was over and everyone was getting ready to leave. Waking up like from a trance, he walked with Kathleen to the door to say goodbye to everyone. As soon as she closed the door, she turned rather quickly and looked at him for a few seconds. "Where in the world is your head? You were a total blank for the last hour. Are you sick or something?"

"No, no," answered Jackie.

"And why do you have that strange smile on your face?" she asked. Together they walked back into the living room and began picking up the empty glasses and trash.

"I know who killed Joey Mons," he said, feeling a rush of excitement and satisfaction he hadn't felt about his job in a very long time.

After explaining things to Kathleen, he said, "I'm going to stay up for a while; I need to think about this some more. And don't worry about cleaning up. I'll take care of it." He kissed Kathleen good night at the foot of stairs, then walked back to the living room. It was a long time before he shut out the lights and headed upstairs.

On Monday Jackie began his shift at 4 p.m. and would work until midnight. He couldn't wait to tell Nick about the weekend. He had practically memorized his conversation with Packie O'Brien. He arrived at the station 15 minutes early, hoping that Nick would be early too. Nick was already sitting at his desk with a cup of coffee in his hand and a newspaper in front of him. Jackie almost burst through the door and proceeded directly to the front of Nick's desk.

"Nick," he said. "Gotta few minutes? I need to run something by you."

"Sure," answered Nick, as he savored the last bit of his honey-dipped donut, folded the paper and dropped it on his desk. "What's so important? You look all wound up."

Jackie sat down and excitedly told Nick about what he had heard from Packie, along with all the other pieces of the puzzle that were now fitting into place. When Jackie finished, Nick leaned forward in his chair and stared at his partner. "Jackie, I think you're finally on to something. It's about time we talked with Phil."

Nick and Jackie discussed the case for the next 30 minutes. The rest of the night was quiet and Jackie left the station about 12:15 a.m. He didn't notice the green sedan which was parked across the street from the station.

Kathleen was in bed but awake when Jackie arrived home. He kissed her and started to undress.

"I'm not really tired yet. How about I make us a cup of tea?" said Jackie.

"Okay, that sounds good. And the chef can make some toast, please."

Jackie came to the bed and gave his wife another kiss.

"Does the chef get a tip?"

Kathleen smiled and gave him another kiss.

Jackie went downstairs to the kitchen and put the water on and popped two slices of bread in the toaster. He made a trip to the bathroom and when he returned the water was boiling and the toast was ready. He put the tea and toast on a tray, along with a knife and a jar of grape jelly, and carried it upstairs to the bedroom. He put the tray on the table where Kathleen could reach it from the bed, then began to undress. While she was eating, Jackie said, "Nick and I talked quite a bit about Phil Merchinson today," and told Kathleen what had been said.

"Sure sounds like a lot of coincidences," she said.

"I know," Jackie answered. "But they're becoming more than just coincidences."

When she had finished eating Jackie took the tray and placed it on the chair by the door, kissed her good night and turned out the light. Neither one heard the green car start or see Phil Merchinson drive away.

Merchinson drove down Main Street, headed toward the Shamrock Club which was near Sullivan Square. He pulled into a parking spot just outside the club entrance. Spider Hayes, Tommy's brother, was on the door so he let Phil in immediately. No words were spoken, just nods of recognition. The Shamrock Club was an after hours club owned by Tommy Hayes. It opened shortly after the famous Stork Club on Chelsea Street was closed down in the early sixties. All drinks were five dollars and at times there were some high stakes card games. Of course, Tommy ran a tight ship and took care of the police. He didn't allow any drugs to be used or sold there, but you could always get an address where you could get anything you wanted.

Tommy was in his small but elaborate office located at the rear of the club. Tony Sapp was with him, counting money from the week's take. Both were using large, noisy calculators. The desk was covered with 10's, 20's and hundred dollar bills. After the money was counted it was taken to a secure place. Only Tommy and Tony Sapp knew the location. Tony was the only guy that Tommy trusted. He had tried to lure Jackie Monyhan into this job, knowing Jackie would be good at it because he was so good in math, but Jackie said he wasn't interested. Plus, with Jackie now a detective, Tommy couldn't afford any scrutiny by the police. At least, the police he didn't otherwise have on the take. Still, he liked Jackie and didn't like what Phil was doing.

Phil went to the bar, sat down on a bar stool and ordered a scotch and soda. He spoke to no one. He just sat staring at his drink. He knew Tommy was in the back room counting money, so he decided to wait a while. He wasn't sure what Tommy wanted to talk to him about, but he had an idea. He was hoping that Tommy didn't know anything about the Joey Mons killing. The only one who knew was Joey-the-Shoes Connolly and Phil had scared him shitless about saying anything about it. But Phil had heard about his drunken exploits at Doherty's last week. Maybe he needed to visit with Joey-the-Shoes real soon and remind him to keep his mouth shut. Still, his name had been mentioned so he had kept a low profile for the next few weeks. Tommy had only used him for special hits. Even many of Tommy's close associates didn't know much about Phil.

After about 15 minutes Phil decided to go to the back room. The drink had calmed him down. The first one always did. Liam Cloughrety, a 350 pounder in a black suit, white shirt and purple tie whose head matched the size of a basketball, with tiny slits for eyes, was sitting in a high stool outside the door. He looked at Phil and said slowly, "I'll let Tommy know you're here." He lumbered out from his chair, turned and knocked quietly a couple times on the door, then entered. Less than a minute later he opened the door and motioned to Phil to come through. Phil waved a silent thanks, then walked into the room. Liam closed the door and returned to his stool.

Phil was no stranger here but it always surprised him how comfortable the room was decorated. It was paneled in dark wood on all four sides which matched the hard wood floors. A large Oriental rug was perfectly aligned in front of Tommy's ornamental, mahogany desk. There were three TV's and a new stereo set on one wall along with a small bar set out on a long table against another wall. Brass table lamps with cream colored shades gave the room a warm glow. On the one wall which fronted the street there were two windows which were covered almost completely by red velvet curtains which reached to the floor. Tommy was sitting behind his neat desk in a dark brown leather chair. He was a sharp dresser and knew it. He felt comfortable in a suit and tie and could easily pass for an executive from Gillette's or Hood's Milk. He stood and walked from behind the desk and shook hands with Phil. He told Phil to take a seat opposite the desk as he returned to his leather chair.

"How is it going?" Tommy asked casually.

"Pretty good," answered Phil confidently. "I have enough money to keep me going and I'm sure you'll have some work for me, which is okay, too."

Tommy smiled. "Yeah, that's one of the reasons I asked you to come over tonight. I need you to talk to someone who is late paying his debts and giving us a hard time."

"Sure, no problem," replied Phil.

"I hear that you had a little trouble recently with some jewelry. Is that all straightened out?"

"Yeah, no problem. No one's going to finger me. Don't worry."

"In any case, after this little job, I want you to take it easy for awhile. I don't want any attention from the cops. You sometimes don't understand that we don't like publicity. We take care of our own, you understand, but the less heat, the better."

"Yeah, okay. I've been wanting to see some friends in Providence anyway. Maybe it's time to make a visit."

"Sounds good. Get in touch when you get back." After a short pause he added, "Oh, and there's something else that has been brought to my attention."

"Oh, what's that?" said Phil, sitting up straighter in his chair, wondering what was coming next.

"No big deal. But I've been hearing that you've been following Jackie Monyhan around. I'd like to know why. He's a friend of mine, even if he is a cop."

"Well," said Phil, settling into his chair again. "I got word that he was asking around about me and I just wanted to see what he looked like, what kind of person he is. That's all. I get a little bit nervous when a cop is asking about me."

"I understand," said Tommy with a somewhat forced smile. "Just keep me informed. Don't make any moves on him, that's all."

No other words were spoken as the two men stared at each other for several seconds. Tommy then reached into the top drawer of his desk and took out a small, unmarked envelope and handed it to Phil. "All the information you need is there. Same fee as before."

Phil nodded, as he casually reached over the desk for the envelope and placed it in his jacket's inside pocket, adding a simple, "Thanks."

The meeting was over.

Phil left the Shamrock Club and drove through Sullivan Square, headed for his apartment in Medford. Few people knew where he lived and he wanted to keep it that way. He felt the envelope that Tommy had given him and smiled. It was nice to get paid for doing something you liked to do. With some fresh cash he thought briefly that he might join up in a polka game with some friends in Providence. Providence was a good city to get lost in.

CHAPTER 15

▼

Phil Merchinson got out of bed at 9 a.m. He made coffee and toast which he ate in the small kitchen off his bedroom. Again, he looked at the instructions and the name of the late payer that Tommy Hayes wanted him to talk to. Phil approached debt collecting in a different way than Charlie Wilson did. Charlie was a brute who tried to intimidate his clients physically, regardless of who they were. But Phil knew that if you broke a longshoreman or a truck driver's arm, then the guy couldn't work. So how was he supposed to get you the money he owed? Phil's approach was much different. He would learn everything about the guy, about his family, about his friends, where he socialized, if he went to church, did he cheat on his wife, did she cheat on him. Where did his children go to school? It was amazing how this knowledge could be used to speed up payments.

The name on the paper was a supervisor at the Boston Globe. He loved to gamble and had been on a losing streak when he borrowed $1000 from Hayes. Like all gamblers, he went to the track thinking he could double or triple his money, thus paying off his debt and having some money left for himself. He was married to a woman who was a nurse at the Witton Memorial in Everett. She made good money but her husband would never see any of it. She knew about his problem and wasn't going to go down the river with him. They had two children that attended a parochial school. Phil realized that threats had to be made in such a way that the guy wouldn't go to the police, but serious enough to force him into paying. Phil thought about the kind of a strategy he would use on this guy. Maybe let some air out of a few tires might be an easy beginning along with a few, late night phone calls. Maybe he'd get the idea without too much work.

It was 2 a.m. and Kathleen was feeling sharp and frequent pains. She was going into labor. She jabbed Jackie in the back, "I think we need to go to the hospital." They waited about an hour, then called Dr. O'Brien and told him what was happening. He said to go to St. Margaret's immediately and he would meet them there.

It only took them 15 minutes to get to St. Margaret's in Dorchester. As always, the hospital was busy. It was the most popular baby hospital in the Boston area. Jackie took care of the registration details as the nurses took Kathleen to a changing room from which she would go to the labor room when necessary. Jackie hesitated in making any phone calls because he knew this could be a false alarm. He headed for the cafeteria to get a cup of coffee. By 6 a.m. nothing had happened so he decided to call Lt. Malvesti and let him know what was going on. Malvesti told him to stay with his wife and call him later. By 9 a.m. the doctor was going to send Kathleen home when the pains set in again and wouldn't stop or slow down. Doctor O'Brien waved Jackie out from the room and told the nurses to take Kathleen into the labor room.

Kathleen gave birth to a somewhat premature, but healthy, 6 lb, 4 ounce boy at 9:51 a.m. The boy would be named John Mark Monyhan. Jackie called his mother and told her the good news. She would call the rest of the family. They would set up a schedule for visiting the hospital so as not to wear out Kathleen. Jackie called work and talked to Lt. Malvesti who said that they could get by without him for a day or two, but if he got bored, he could come in anytime. After about an hour, Jackie got to hold his son for the first time.

Kathleen was in the hospital for five days before she and Jack, Jr. came home. Jackie had the bedroom set up so the basinet would fit next to their bed. He was on the midnight shift this week, but fortunately, the baby was sleeping half the night. This was a break for Kathleen, too. Gradually, she was getting back her energy.

On Friday night of that same week Tommy Hayes received a call from Phil Merchinson.

"Tommy, it's Phil. Just wanted to let you know that that job you wanted me to fix is all set. You'll be getting payment for it by tomorrow, the latest."

"Glad to hear it, Phil. I knew I could count on you."

"Yeah, no problem, any time. Look, I'm going out of town for a few days, but if you need anything when I get back, just give me a call."

Okay, thanks for letting me know. Give my regards to whoever," Tommy added with a smile. Phil didn't answer as he hung up the phone.

Tommy waited a few seconds, then picked up the phone and dialed a number. "Hi, it's me. Our schedule's moved up a bit. Can you talk?"

CHAPTER 16

▼

On his way to Providence, Phil stopped at a gas station along route 95 and used a pay phone to call Tony Melia, a member of the Providence Grasso Family. He set up a meeting with him for the next day. Tony had a small job for Phil to do. It would only take a day but the fee would be high. He then drove to the Blue Moon Hotel on the Providence water front and booked a room for the night. He showered and dressed before he went out to dinner. He knew of a fine Italian restaurant on Border Street. It was just a short walk from the Blue Moon.

Shortly after 7 p.m. he entered the Olive Tree Restaurant and found a seat at the back of the dining room. He wasn't worried, but he liked to have a clear view of his surroundings. He ordered a small antipasto, veal piccata and a glass of Chianti. Phil liked wine and was quite the connoisseur. He liked living the high life, which included enjoying good food, expensive wine and attractive women. Tonight he could relax and enjoy himself, concentrating on the present and not worrying about the past or future. He liked this place. The decorations were a bit over the top with the plastic grapes draped from the low ceiling along with the gaudy paintings of partially nude men and women on just about every wall, but it was quiet and the service, as usual, was efficient. No one knew him here by name, only as a repeat customer, which he appreciated. Getting his favorite table near the back was now almost automatic.

As he ate, he didn't notice the well-built young man who came in the front entrance and sat at the bar. He had on a black leather coat and scally cap which he didn't bother to take off. The man ordered a beer, then took a package of Camels from his shirt pocket. He hit the unopened package several times on the bar to settle them. He opened the package and withdrew one, then placed the pack on the bar in front of him. As he held the cigarette between his lips he struggled somewhat to pull out a lighter from his pants pocket. He lit the cigarette while taking the first draw deeply into his lungs. As he exhaled toward the ceiling he turned to face the TV but his eyes were also scanning the dining room. When he spotted Phil Merchinson, a small, hardly noticeable smile appeared on his face.

Jackie was scheduled to work the late shift that night when he got a call from Nick around 6:30 p.m.

"Jackie, you need to get down here right away. We've got some good information on Phil Merchinson and we need to get on it right away."

"I'll be right down." Grabbing his coat and gun he hurried upstairs and told Kathleen that he needed to go to the station right away.

"I'll call you when I know more. Don't hold supper for me." They embraced quickly and before Jackie could leave, Kathleen whispered in his ear.

"I love you, you know. Be careful."

"Don't worry. This could be the break we've been waiting for." He hurried down the steps and to his car.

Twenty minutes later Jackie met Nick coming from their office with his coat on and a fist full of papers in his hand.

"Let's go. I'll explain it on the way. You take the wheel."

"Where're we going, can you tell me that?" Jackie asked as he hurried to join Nick heading down the stairs.

"Providence," answered Nick.

Once in the car, Jackie was full of questions, but Nick was the first to talk.

"We got a call from someone that Phil was probably going to Providence today. He has friends there. The caller also gave us the name of Phil's favorite restaurant in town." Nick shuffled through his papers. "A place called the Olive Tree. Guess it's Italian by the sound."

"Yeah," answered Jackie. "I know where it is. It's not too far from the waterfront. I used to go down to the docks in Providence once and awhile. I'm surprised the place is still in business. It's secluded. Sounds like a place a hood would want to hang out." A few seconds later Jackie asked, "You believe this guy who called?"

"Yeah, it sounds good. The call came in upstairs. Seems that Phil isn't well liked by a lot of people, including the crowd that he works for."

"We've got nothing to lose anyway," said Jackie, as he managed to run a yellow light before turning onto the entrance ramp to the Southeast Expressway. They drove in the high speed lane through Milton, Quincy and Braintree, then made the tight turn onto Route 95 heading south toward Providence. The traffic at this time of the day was heavy with rush hour traffic. They exited the first ramp into Providence about 50 minutes later. Jackie headed toward the waterfront.

About a dozen more people entered the dining room. Phil finished his meal and ordered an espresso with a cannoli for dessert. He wanted a cigar but decided to wait until he walked back to the Blue Moon. During this time, the young man at the bar had ordered another beer and drank it slowly. He appeared to be deep in thought, occasionally looking up at the TV. Phil paid his bill, exchanged small talk with the waitress whom he seemed to know, then got up and headed for the men's room. The man at the bar put his cigarettes in his shirt pocket, paid his tab along with an adequate tip, stood up and walked out the front door. His car was parked at the rear of the restaurant's parking lot. He started his car but kept the headlights off. There was no way Phil could see him when he came out the front door to walk back to his hotel.

Jackie checked his watch. It was 8:10 p.m. The traffic had slowed once they had exited onto the ramp. They inched along, making every red light, unwilling to put the flashing blue light on the roof which could alert Phil and maybe his friends. After making several turns on the local streets they saw the sign that the waterfront was straight ahead. There were no other cars on the road. At 8:22 p.m. Jackie saw the sign for Mellivele Street, knowing that it would lead directly to the Olive Tree.

Phil came out of the restaurant, stopped just outside the door, took a cigar from his inside pocket and lighted it with his dependable Zippo lighter. He crossed the street, enjoying the cool, clear air and the first few puffs of his cigar. At 8:20 p.m. there was very little traffic in this part of the city and the sidewalks were empty, except for Phil, now walking rather slowly on the other side of the street.

The man put the car in gear and drove slowly toward the front of the lot. He looked both ways, then turned right onto the street. He saw Phil about 100 feet ahead of him on the opposite sidewalk. Phil heard the car approach and wondered why the car didn't pick up speed but was just coasting. He turned to his right to look and thought of reaching for his gun, but it was too late. He turned to face the car, with his hand starting to go for the inside of his jacket, just as Salvatore Mons pulled the trigger three times. Two of the bullets hit Phil on his left side, close to his heart. The third entered closer to his intestines. Phil fell backward, clutching his stomach. He was dead before he hit the pavement, the lit cigar still glowing on the sidewalk next to his outstretched hand.

As their car turned the corner they immediately saw the small, lighted sign for the Olive Tree on the right hand side of the street, some 100 yards away. Jackie could feel his heart beating much faster now. Nervously, Jackie and Nick scanned the area for anything suspicious. The narrow street was lined with mostly old warehouses and empty lots. Nick broke the silence.

"Kind of an out of the way place to have a restaurant."

"That's probably why Phil likes it so much," said Jackie. As the car moved slowly toward the restaurant, they saw about 20 people grouped together just outside the door. Otherwise the neighborhood appeared to be deserted.

"Why are there so many people just standing outside the restaurant?" wondered Nick. "Is the food that good?" he asked, half joking. Jackie pulled the car over to the curb and shut off the engine, then the head lights.

"Something isn't right," said Jackie. "They all seem to be looking down the street at something."

Jackie and Nick approached cautiously, pushing their way through the crowd.

"What's going on here?" asked Nick. "We're police."

Someone in the crowd answered, "Somebody got shot. Just a few minutes ago. We just called the police. You sure got here fast."

The crowd opened up and Jackie and Nick walked through. The body on the ground was not moving. With guns drawn, the detectives moved closer, bent over the body and checked the pulse of the outstretched hand. They also tried for a pulse in his neck. They heard the sound of sirens approaching. All Jackie could do was look at Nick and say, "It's him. And he's dead."

The Providence police arrived and quickly moved the spectators back. One of them yelled to everyone in the crowd, "Everybody stay where you are. Nobody leaves. We need to get your names and addresses." Jackie and Nick stood up and pulled out their badges.

"Who the hell are you guys?" one barked before the detectives could say a word.

"Monyhan and Solomonte, Boston police," answered Nick. "Who are you?"

"Officer Shapiro. We got a call that someone had been shot." Approaching the body on the ground he asked, "Is the guy dead?"

"Yeah. No vital signs. We got a tip and came down here to arrest him. Looks like somebody else was looking for him, too."

"Who is he?" Shapiro asked, getting closer to the body.

"His name's Phil Merchinson; belonged to one of Boston's mobs. We've been waiting a long time for a break in a murder case. We finally got lucky tonight."

"Looks like someone just saved you a lot of trouble," replied Shapiro, bending over the body.

"Yeah," replied Jackie. It was the only thing that he could manage to say.

"Mind if we stick around and find out if anybody saw anything?" asked Nick. By this time Officer Shapiro had calmed down.

"No, glad to be of service," Shapiro answered with a smile.

After working with the Providence police interviewing witnesses and people in the restaurant for the next two hours, Jackie and Nick arrived back in Charlestown around 11 p.m. Nick had driven while Jackie had used the time to write some notes on what had happened. They still had to make out a detailed report but both agreed that it could wait until they each had gotten something to eat and some sleep.

Around midnight Jackie unlocked his front door. It was quiet. Kathleen had left a few lights on in the living room and kitchen. After taking off his coat and throwing it on the chair, Jackie went into the kitchen and opened the refrigerator. He was surprised that he wasn't hungry, only thirsty. Reaching for the quart of milk he heard the sound of slippers behind him. Jackie turned to Kathleen and gave her a tired smile.

"You want me to get you anything? Have you had anything to eat?" asked Kathleen, sounding concerned.

"No, thanks. I just need something to drink. I feel okay, just tired."

Jackie took his glass of milk and sat at the kitchen table. Kathleen sat down across from him.

"We closed the Joey Mons case tonight. After all these years, we finally closed the book on it." He paused before adding, "But we got there too late. Someone beat us to it. By only minutes, too."

"Was it that Merchinson guy? The one that you've suspected for a long time?"

"Yes. Someone was waiting for him to come out of a restaurant in Providence. We questioned some witnesses but there's nothing really to go on."

"Any idea who might have done it?"

"No. There were only two witnesses who just happened to come out of the restaurant a few seconds before Phil got shot. And they both gave pretty much the same statement. The three shots came from the driver's side of a dark sedan with its light off and the person at the wheel had yelled out the window, "That one's for Joey.""

CHAPTER 17

▼

Jackie sat at his desk and reread their final report several times. Phil Merchinson had been murdered, after all this time. But who had done it? Phil had a lot of enemies, including friends and relatives of those he had killed or tormented. But Jackie knew that the police wouldn't spend much time or effort to solve this case, and he wasn't going to either. Several names came to mind, but since it happened in Providence, he wasn't going to push it. One name kept nagging at him, however. He made up his mind that the next time, if there ever was a next time, that he saw Joey's brother, Sal, he might just want to sit down and have a friendly chat. With no strings attached.

A smile crept over Jackie's face. For now, it was like a chain had been broken; now Jackie had been set free. Although he wasn't the one who delivered the final blow, nevertheless he felt as if he had.

But for Kathleen and him it was worth a celebration. Italian food and a bottle of wine, expensive wine, Jackie said to himself with a silent laugh. Joey would have loved that. He took a key from his pocket, inserted it in his bottom desk drawer and opened it. He took out three folders and wrapped a large elastic band around them, along with a 3 x 5 index card which he taped on top. He took a pen and wrote "CLOSED" on the index card, taking pleasure while writing each letter slowly and deliberately. As he put the folders back into the drawer he heard the Captain holler, "Monyhan and Solomonte. There's been a shooting at Town Field. Get on it, now!" After waiting a few seconds spent staring at the folders, Jackie rose quickly from his chair and kicked the drawer shut.

978-0-595-42732-1
0-595-42732-4